CONTINUE THE MISSION

WE THE PEOPLE'S HANDBOOK

GREGG C. CUMMINGS

U.S. ARMY VETERAN, LEO VETERAN
FOUNDER OF CONTINUETHEMISSION.NET

TABLE OF CONTENTS

INTRODUCTION: 6

PATRIOTS CREED   9

DECLARATION OF INDEPENDENCE   11

CONSTITUTION OF THE UNITED STATES   18

BILL OF RIGHTS   35

A GUIDE TO COMMUNICATIONS

AND NETWORKING   51

-WORD OF MOUTH COMMUNICATION TECHNIQUE   51

-OTHER MEANS OF COMMUNICATION

AND THEIR BEST PRACTICES   59

    -NEWS PAPER

    -PHONE

    -EMAIL

    -SOCIAL MEDIA

    -WEBSITES

    -TALK RADIO

    -TELEVISION NEWS

STARTING AND OPERATING A WE THE PEOPLE GROUP   70

    -INTRODUCTION

    -CREATE AN ORGANIZING COMMITTEE

    -GROUP NAME AND PURPOSE

    -MISSION STATEMENT

    -ESTABLISH AN ORGANIZATION

    -DEVELOP AN IMAGE

    -CONNECT TO OTHER GRASSROOT GROUPS

    -COMMUNICATIONS OF GROUP

    -GETTING MEMBERS AND ENCOURAGING OTHERS

    -FUNDING

    -FUNDING EVENTS

    -OTHER AREAS TO CONSIDER

KEY UNDERSTANDINGS "WE THE PEOPLE" MUST KNOW   82

    -SANTA MARIA VS MAYFLOWER

    -DEMOCRACY VS REPUBLIC

    -DIVERSITY VS UNIVERSITY

    -IROQUOIS IN CONSTITUTION

    -ELECTORAL COLLEGE

WHY IS PREPPING/SURVIVAL

SIGNIFICANT FOR WE THE PEOPLE?   96

    -WHAT EXACTLY IS PREPPING?

    -WHY IS IT IMPORTANT? (COMPLACENCY/SLOTHFULNESS/

    SPOLED IS A HINT)

    -WHEN IS THE RIGHT TIME TO START?

    -SOME BASICS TO GET STARTED

    CONSTITUTIONAL MILITIA SOLUTION   102

    -STRUCTURE AND INDIVIDUAL ROLES AND

    RESPONSIBILITIES

    -TRAINING

    -PUBLIC RELATIONS

FOUNDATIONAL INFORMATION NEEDED   107

1776 PROJECT COMMISSION REPORT

FORWARD

Why this We The People's Handbook? With the ever growing, and absolute purpose driven lack of education on our American history, the very essence of E Pluribus Unum (from the many one) is being forgotten, eroded, and manipulated out of existence. This is no made up theory, but a direct in your face disregard for the importance of our founders original intent of a free nation. Our beloved Republic has witnessed a blatant systematic campaign by the local, state, and federal government to tear down any belief or revered education on our Declaration of Independence, Constitution, or Bill of Rights. The sacredness of these documents, our US Flag, and the true focus of Unity of the people, has all but been diluted with ideological government systems that have always been in direct opposition to the United States of America. Ideologies like a pure democracy, socialism, Marxism, fascism, and communism, which all fall under one umbrella of modern day globalism.

This is not new, this slow frog boil has been going on for decades.

Generation after generation our minds have been clouded, and purposely not fed truth in history, nor educated in the authority of the people within our Republic. Do not hide from the fact that the degradation of our nations flag, the division of the American people, and the replacement of authority of our Constitution, are the premier goals of modern day globalism, using progressivism as the tool to get them there.

You see to restore the honor in our nation's flag. To bring true university in We The People. To ensure we strengthen and maintain the law of our Republic, the Constitution of the United States. We the people need to defend our liberties and reestablish our freedoms under God by first and foremost uniting as one people through our education, understanding that our Republic as laid out in our Constitution is key to making America better than it has ever been. We must find the tools, techniques and best practices to stand up against detached governmental powers and the controls of influence they have in media and entertainment. We The People must wake up and see the hypocritical manipulations that are being forced upon our children in the form of indoctrinations.

All of the above is 100% truth, 100% in our faces, and 100% been a gradual growth of cancer that has fundamentally changed our Republic into a national socialist democracy. I believe this handbook is not only needed, but crucial in an ever closing window of opportunity that We the people have left to save the United States of America.

May God bless each of you, may each of you grow in character, and may all the citizens of the U.S.A. unite as One People, One Nation, to continue to pursue the American dream.

"Charlie Mike" (Continue the Mission)

Gregg C. Cummings

Founder of Continuethemission.net

INTRODUCTION

Deep within the woodlands, a young female warrior from days past is on a hunt. A hunt that she prepared for all her life, a sacred hunt that is a quest to enlightenment. She does not know what is in store for her, she only knows that it is time to stand up, and hunt. Unlike most of her expeditions, tonight she hunts by the light of a new moon. Snow is falling in large flakes, her breath visibly leading the way with each breath she exhales, as the silence of this cold still night seems to guide her direction, almost magnetizing her steps in the fresh fallen, soft and powdery snow. As she walks through these tall and strong birch trees, watching, listening as she continues to seek out any life or tracks of possible prey. Then it happens, time, yes her actual existence seems to stop all around her. She senses it, so she kneels with her axe tip stabbed slightly in the snow at her feet. Then it happened, a feeling engulfing her spirit as she glares deep between the trees in front of her and she sees a direct moon beam of light directly shining on what seems as a skinned bound book lying on a rock. A truly magical sight as the book seemed to almost be asking to be found on this cold night, it glowed bright reflecting the light around it.

The female warrior approached the book looking over her shoulders to see if it might be tied to anyone around close by, listening for the slightest of movement other than her own, but there was no one, only silence and a small whistle as the wind blew through the forest arounds her. Now standing in front of the book, she picked it up and began to read by the moonlight, pacing back and forth and reading some more as she sat down, and continued to read, and read some more she did. Before she knew it she finished the book in what appeared to be just an hour or so, but she actually read till the moon vanished and the rising sun brought a new beginning to her eyes. She then shut the back cover of the book, she stood up and looked to her right and sees you. Yes you reading this book right now. Somehow as she finished this book she magically knew her purpose, her mission is to present this to you. So hear, hear this vital message from her own words.

"Come with me,

Come with me on a journey and that very much connects you individually as well as we the people collectively.

First let me introduce myself, I am Yggdrasker. I am a strong spirited female warrior very much saturated by the Spirit of America.

I grew up knowing I was free, free to live, speak and dream. So dream I did. Today our lives, voices and dreams are being snuffed out by an ever growing corrupt government with one mission. "Control".

We have sat idle and watched, or even worse, ignored our rights within our liberties be ripped from our very grasp by global elitists and communist with a one world agenda at hand. "Control"

When is enough enough. When do we stand and fight for our rights to live, fight for our children's rights to dream. Stand up with determined focus to fight to be free.

Now is the time! Now we stand! Now we fight!

We are dogs no more, today we become lions!

In my hand I hold the very foundation of We The People. I hold a weapon that will help destroy the enemy. If we but choose to unite as one. It will teach you why to fight, when to fight, and how to function in this dangerous society.

7

And above all it'll teach you how to become free again and stay free!

Come, Come with me..."

"...You see every warrior, every knight, and every patriot must be bound to a set of beliefs which guides their actions each and every day. This Patriot Creed before you, is just such a set of beliefs. It is no wonder why this was the first document within this blessed text, read it, understand it, and live by it my brothers and sisters, as your future depends on it. Our future as one people, depends on your commitment and your sacred honor."

PATRIOT CREED

<u>P</u>assionately I dedicated myself as a Patriot, knowing full well the position I place myself within our nation today, I will always stand up, speak out, and defend the foundation of this one nation under God.

<u>A</u>cknowledging the fact that a Patriot will always lead by example the Patriotism, Morality, and Faith that so many had done before me.

<u>T</u>esting my intestinal fortitude in the face of the enemy as I step forward always to stand my ground and shield the sacred documents of my country.

<u>R</u>emembering always those that gave the ultimate price so that we may live free with liberty and someday witness the outcome that our forefathers envisioned.

<u>I</u>dentifying the need of my fellow countrymen I will shoulder more than my share of the task to always stoke the movement with strength and momentum to accomplish the mission.

<u>O</u>bjectively will I assess all mankind individually by their character, their traits, and their actions of citizenship.

<u>T</u>aking into account the importance of accountability of myself and that of my elected officials, so that our country might operate as the blessing of equality and prosperity for generations to come.

Gregg C. Cummings 2012

"Here is the beginning, a new turn not only for the people of this great nation but for the development of true light in the world for all of humankind, this leads with courage to stand up to your oppressor, to actually create your freedom and liberty that translates to an action taken and becoming independent from tyranny and suppression. Know your beginning, and the explanation of your foundation, then you will understand the ideology that maintains that unity and oneness. Read and understand..."

THE DECLARATION OF INDEPENDENCE

Action of Second Continental Congress, July 4, 1776 The Unanimous Declaration of the thirteen united States of America

When in the Course of human events, it becomes necessary for one People to dissolve the Political Bands which have connected them with another, and to assume among the Powers of the earth, the separate and equal Station to which the Laws of Nature and of Nature's God entitle them, a decent Respect to the Opinions of Mankind requires that they should declare the causes which impel them to the Separation.

We hold these Truths to be self-evident, that all Men are created equal, that they are endowed by their Creator with certain unalienable Rights, that among these are Life, Liberty, and the pursuit of happiness—That to secure these Rights, Governments are instituted among Men, deriving

11

their just Powers from the Consent of the Governed, that whenever any Form of Government becomes destructive of these ends, it is the Right of the People to alter or to abolish it, and to institute new Government, laying its Foundation on such Principles, and organizing its Powers in such Form, as to them shall seem most likely to effect their Safety and happiness. Prudence, indeed, will dictate that Governments long established should not be changed for light and transient Causes; and accordingly all experience hath shewn, that Mankind are more disposed to suffer, while evils are sufferable, than to right themselves by abolishing the Forms to which they are accustomed. But when a long Train of Abuses and Usurpations, pursuing invariably the same Object, evinces a design to reduce them under absolute Despotism, it is their Right, it is their Duty, to throw off such Government, and to provide new Guards for their future Security. Such has been the patient Sufferance of these Colonies; and such is now the Necessity which constrains them to alter their former Systems of Government. The history of the present King of Great-Britain is a history of repeated Injuries and Usurpations, all having in direct Object the establishment of an absolute Tyranny over these States. To prove this, let Facts be submitted to a candid World.

He has refused his Assent to Laws, the most wholesome and necessary for the public Good.

He has forbidden his Governors to pass Laws of immediate and pressing Importance, unless suspended in their Operation till his Assent should be obtained; and when so suspended, he has utterly neglected to attend to them.

He has refused to pass other Laws for the Accommodation of large Districts of People, unless those People would relinquish the Right of Representation in the Legislature, a Right inestimable to them, and formidable to Tyrants only.

He has called together Legislative Bodies at Places unusual, uncomfortable, and distant from the Depository of their public Records, for the sole Purpose of fatiguing them into Compliance with his Measures.

He has dissolved Representative houses repeatedly, for opposing with manly Firmness his Invasions on the Rights of the People.

He has refused for a long Time, after such Dissolutions, to cause others to be elected; whereby the Legislative Powers, incapable of Annihilation, have returned to the People at large for their exercise; the State remaining in the mean time exposed to all the Dangers of Invasion from without, and Convulsions within.

He has endeavoured to prevent the Population of these States; for that Purpose obstructing the Laws for Naturalization of Foreigners; refusing to pass others to encourage their Migrations hither, and raising the Conditions of new Appropriations of Lands.

He has obstructed the Administration of Justice, by refusing his Assent to Laws for establishing Judiciary Powers.

He has made Judges dependent on his Will alone, for the Tenure of their Offices, and the Amount and Payment of their Salaries.

He has erected a Multitude of new Offices, and sent hither Swarms of Officers to harrass our People, and eat out their Substance.

He has kept among us, in Times of Peace, Standing Armies, without the consent of our Legislatures.

He has affected to render the Military independent of and superior to the Civil Power.

He has combined with others to subject us to a Jurisdiction foreign to our Constitution, and unacknowledged by our Laws; giving his Assent to their Acts of pretended Legislation:

For quartering large Bodies of Armed Troops among us:

For protecting them, by a mock Trial, from Punishment for any Murders which they should commit on the Inhabitants of these States:

For cutting off our Trade with all Parts of the World:

For imposing Taxes on us without our Consent:

For depriving us, in many Cases, of the Benefits of Trial by Jury:

For transporting us beyond Seas to be tried for pretended Offences:

For abolishing the free System of english Laws in a neighbouring Province, establishing therein an arbitrary Government, and enlarging its Boundaries, so as to render it at once an example and fit Instrument for introducing the same absolute Rule into these Colonies:

For taking away our Charters, abolishing our most valuable Laws, and altering fundamentally the Forms of our Governments:

For suspending our own Legislatures, and declaring themselves invested with Power to legislate for us in all Cases whatsoever.

He has abdicated Government here, by declaring us out of his Protection and waging War against us.

He has plundered our Seas, ravaged our Coasts, burnt our Towns, and destroyed the Lives of our People.

He is, at this Time, transporting large Armies of foreign Mercenaries to compleat the Works of Death, Desolation, and Tyranny, already begun with circumstances of Cruelty and Perfidy, scarcely paralleled in the most barbarous Ages, and totally unworthy the head of a civilized Nation.

He has constrained our fellow Citizens taken Captive on the high Seas to bear Arms against their Country, to become the executioners of their Friends and Brethren, or to fall themselves by their hands.

He has excited domestic Insurrections amongst us, and has endeavoured to bring on the Inhabitants of our Frontiers, the merciless Indian Savages, whose known Rule of Warfare, is an undistinguished Destruction of all Ages, Sexes and Conditions.

In every stage of these Oppressions we have Petitioned for Redress in the most humble Terms: Our repeated Petitions have been answered only by repeated Injury. A Prince, whose Character is thus marked by every act which may define a Tyrant, is unfit to be the Ruler of a free People.

Nor have we been wanting in Attentions to our British Brethren. We have warned them from Time to Time of Attempts by their Legislature to extend an unwarrantable Jurisdiction over us. We have reminded them of the Circumstances of our emigration and Settlement here. We have appealed to their native Justice and Magnanimity, and we have conjured them by the Ties of our common Kindred to disavow these Usurpations, which, would inevitably interrupt our Connections and Correspondence. They too have been deaf to the Voice of Justice and of Consanguinity. We must, therefore, acquiesce in the Necessity, which denounces our Separation, and hold them, as we hold the rest of Mankind, enemies in War, in Peace, Friends.

We, therefore, the Representatives of the united States of America, in General Congress, Assembled, appealing to the Supreme Judge of the World for the Rectitude of our Intentions, do, in the Name, and by Authority of the good People of these Colonies, solemnly Publish and Declare, That these United Colonies are, and of Right ought to be Free and Independent States; that they are absolved from all Allegiance to the British Crown, and that all political Connection between them and the State of Great-Britain, is and ought to be totally dissolved; and that as Free and Independent States, they have full Power to levy War, conclude Peace, contract Alliances, establish Commerce, and to do all other Acts and Things which Independent States may of right do. —And for the support of this Declaration, with a firm Reliance on the Protection of divine Providence, we mutually pledge to each other our Lives, our Fortunes, and our sacred honor.

Signed by order and in behalf of the Congress,

John Hancock, President Attest.
Charles Thompson, Secretary

Signers of the Declaration of Independence

Georgia:

Button Gwinnett

Lyman Hall

George Walton

North Carolina:

William Hooper

Joseph Hewes

John Penn

South Carolina:

Edward Rutledge

Thomas Heyward,

Jr. Thomas Lynch,

Jr. Arthur Middleton

Massachusetts:

Samuel Adams John Adams

Robert Treat Paine Elbridge Gerry John Hancock

Maryland:

Samuel Chase
William Paca
Thomas Stone
Charles Carroll of Carrollton

Virginia:

George Wythe Richard henry Lee Thomas Jefferson Benjamin Harrison
Thomas Nelson, Jr. Francis Lightfoot Lee Carter Braxton

Pennsylvania:

Robert Morris Benjamin Rush

Benjamin Franklin John Morton George Clymer James Smith George
Taylor James Wilson George Ross

Delaware:

Caesar Rodney George Read Thomas McKean

New York:

William Floyd Philip Livingston Francis Lewis Lewis Morris

New Jersey:

Richard Stockton John Witherspoon Francis Hopkinson John hart
Abraham Clark

New Hampshire:

Josiah Bartlett Matthew Thornton William Whipple

Rhode Island:

Stephen Hopkins William Ellery

Connecticut:

Roger Sherman Samuel Huntington William Williams Oliver Wolcott

"Now this, this is law. This is most sacred and rule of all that guides your people. This, this supreme law of your land tells the government what it CANNOT do to the inhabitance of this land, to those who call themselves American. It is NOT written to show the submissiveness of the citizens, but quite the opposite. The founders wanted to make sure the readers knew who the authority of the government was, that is why they wrote them in very large letters. We The People. Read, and defend your law..."

THE CONSTITUTION OF THE
UNITED STATES

We the People *of the United States*

in Order to form a more perfect Union, establish Justice, insure domestic Tranquility, provide for the common defence, promote the general Welfare, and secure the Blessings of Liberty to ourselves and our Posterity, do ordain and establish this Constitution for the United States of America.

Article I

SECTION. 1.

All legislative Powers herein granted shall be vested in a Congress of the United States, which shall consist of a Sen- ate and House of Representatives.

SECTION. 2.

The House of Representatives shall be composed of Members chosen every second Year by the People of the several States, and the Electors in each State shall have the Qualifications requisite for Electors of the most numerous Branch of the State Legislature.

No Person shall be a Representative who shall not have attained to the Age of twenty five Years, and been seven Years a Citizen of the United States, and who shall not, when elected, be an Inhabitant of that State in which he shall be chosen.

[Representatives and direct Taxes shall be apportioned among the several States which may be included within this Union, according to their respective Numbers, which shall be determined by adding to the whole Number of free Persons, including those bound to Service for a Term of Years, and excluding Indians not taxed, three fifths of all other Persons.]* The actual Enumeration shall be made

within three Years after the first Meeting of the Congress of the United States, and within every subsequent Term of ten Years, in such Manner as they shall by Law direct. The Number of Representatives shall not exceed one for every thirty Thousand, but each State shall have at Least one Representative; and until such enumeration shall be made, the State of New Hampshire shall be entitled to chuse three, Massachusetts eight, Rhode-Island and Providence Plantations one, Connecticut five, New-York six, New Jersey four, Pennsylvania eight, Delaware one, Maryland six, Virginia ten, North Carolina five, South Carolina five, and Georgia three.

When vacancies happen in the Representation from any State, the Executive Authority thereof shall issue Writs of Election to fill such Vacancies.

The House of Representatives shall chuse their Speaker and other Officers; and shall have the sole Power of Impeachment.

The Senate of the United States shall be composed of two Senators from each State, [chosen by the Legislature there- of,]* for six Years; and each Senator shall have one Vote.

Immediately after they shall be assembled in Consequence of the first Election, they shall be divided as equally as may be into three Classes. The Seats of the Senators of the first Class shall be vacated at the Expiration of the second Year, of the second Class at the Expiration of the fourth Year, and of the third Class at the Expiration of the sixth Year, so that one third may be chosen every second Year; [and if Vacancies happen by Resignation, or otherwise, during the Recess of the Legislature of any State, the Executive thereof may make temporary Appointments until the next Meeting of the Legislature, which shall then fill such Vacancies.]*

No Person shall be a Senator who shall not have attained to the Age of thirty Years, and been nine Years a Citizen of the United States, and who shall not, when elected, be an Inhabitant of that State for which he shall be chosen.

The Vice President of the United States shall be President of the Senate, but shall have no Vote, unless they be equally divided.

The Senate shall chuse their other Officers, and also a President pro tempore, in the Absence of the Vice President, or when he shall exercise the Office of President of the United States.

The Senate shall have the sole Power to try all Impeachments. When sitting for that Purpose, they shall be on Oath or Affirmation. When the President of the United States is tried, the Chief Justice shall preside: And no Person shall be convicted without the Concurrence of two thirds of the Members present.

Judgment in Cases of Impeachment shall not extend further than to removal from Office, and disqualification to hold and enjoy any Office of honor, Trust or Profit under the United States: but the Party convicted shall nevertheless be liable and subject to Indictment, Trial, Judgment and Punishment, according to Law.

SECTION. 4.

The Times, Places and Manner of holding Elections for Senators and Representatives, shall be prescribed in each State by the Legislature thereof; but the Congress may at any time by Law make or alter such Regulations, except as to the Places of chusing Senators.

The Congress shall assemble at least once in every Year, and such Meeting shall be [on the first Monday in December,]* unless they shall by Law appoint a different Day.

SECTION. 5.

Each House shall be the Judge of the Elections, Returns and Qualifications of its own Members, and a Majority of each shall constitute a Quorum to do Business; but a smaller Number may adjourn from day to day, and may be authorized to compel the Attendance of absent Members, in such Manner, and under such Penalties as each House may provide.

Each House may determine the Rules of its Proceedings, punish its Members for disorderly Behaviour, and, with the Concurrence of two thirds, expel a Member.

Each House shall keep a Journal of its Proceedings, and from time to time publish the same, excepting such Parts as may in their Judgment require Secrecy; and the Yeas and Nays of the Members of either House on any question shall, at the Desire of one fifth of those Present, be entered on the Journal.

Neither House, during the Session of Congress, shall, with- out the Consent of the other, adjourn for more than three days, nor to any other Place than that in which the two Houses shall be sitting.

SECTION. 6.

The Senators and Representatives shall receive a Compensation for their Services, to be ascertained by Law, and paid out of the Treasury of the United States. They shall in all Cases, except

Treason, Felony and Breach of the Peace, be privileged from Arrest during their Attendance at the Session of their respective Houses, and in going to and returning from the same; and for any Speech or Debate in either House, they shall not be questioned in any other Place.

No Senator or Representative shall, during the Time for which he was elected, be appointed to any civil Office under the Authority of the United States, which shall have been created, or the Emoluments whereof shall have been encreased during such time; and no Person holding any Office under the United States, shall be a Member of either House during his Continuance in Office.

SECTION. 7.

All Bills for raising Revenue shall originate in the House of Representatives; but the Senate may propose or concur with Amendments as on other Bills.

Every Bill which shall have passed the House of Representatives and the Senate, shall, before it become a Law, be presented to the President of the United States; If he approve he shall sign it, but if not he shall return it, with his Objections to that House in which it shall have originated, who shall enter the Objections at large on their Journal, and proceed to reconsider it. If after such Reconsideration two thirds of that House shall agree to pass the Bill, it shall be sent, together with the Objections, to the other House, by which it shall likewise be reconsidered, and if approved by two thirds of that House, it shall become a Law. But in all such Cases the Votes of both Houses shall be determined by Yeas and Nays, and the Names of the Persons voting for and against the Bill shall be entered on the Journal of each House respectively, If any Bill shall not be returned by the President within ten Days (Sundays excepted) after it shall have been presented to him, the Same shall be a Law, in like Manner as if he had signed it, unless the Congress by their Adjournament prevent its Return, in which Case it shall not be a Law.

Every Order, Resolution, or Vote to which the Concurrence of the Senate and House of Representatives may be necessary (except on a question of Adjournment) shall be presented to the President of the United States; and before the Same shall take Effect, shall be approved by him, or being disapproved by him, shall be repassed by two thirds of the Senate and House of Representatives, according to the Rules and Limitations prescribed in the Case of a Bill.

SECTION. 8.

The Congress shall have Power To lay and collect Taxes, Duties, Imposts and Excises, to pay the Debts and provide for the common Defence and general Welfare of the United States; but all Duties, Imposts and Excises shall be uniform throughout the United States;

To borrow Money on the credit of the United States;

To regulate Commerce with foreign Nations, and among the several States, and with the Indian Tribes;

To establish an uniform Rule of Naturalization, and uniform Laws on the subject of Bankruptcies throughout the United States;

To coin Money, regulate the Value thereof, and of foreign Coin, and fix the Standard of Weights and Measures;

To provide for the Punishment of counterfeiting the Securities and current Coin of the United States;

To establish Post Offices and post Roads;
To promote the Progress of Science and useful Arts, by securing for limited Times to Authors and Inventors the exclusive Right to their respective Writings and Discoveries;

To constitute Tribunals inferior to the supreme Court;

To define and punish Piracies and Felonies committed on the high Seas, and Offenses against the Law of Nations;

To declare War, grant Letters of Marque and Reprisal, and make Rules concerning Captures on Land and Water;

To raise and support Armies, but no Appropriation of Money to that Use shall be for a longer Term than two Years;

To provide and maintain a Navy;

To make Rules for the Government and Regulation of the land and naval Forces;

To provide for calling forth the Militia to execute the Laws of the Union, suppress Insurrections and repel Invasions;

To provide for organizing, arming, and disciplining, the Militia, and for governing such Part of them as may be employed in the Service of the United States, reserving to the States respectively, the Appointment of the Officers, and the Authority of training the Militia according to the discipline prescribed by Congress;

To exercise exclusive Legislation in all Cases whatsoever, over such District (not exceeding ten Miles square) as may, by Cession of particular States, and the Acceptance of Congress, become the Seat of the Government of the United States, and to exercise like Authority over all Places purchased by the Consent of the Legislature of the State in which the Same shall be, for the Erection of Forts, Magazines, Arsenals, dock-Yards and other needful Buildings; -And

To make all Laws which shall be necessary and proper for carrying into Execution the foregoing Powers, and all other Powers vested by this Constitution in the Government of the United States, or in any Department or Officer thereof.

SECTION. 9.

The Migration or Importation of such Persons as any of the States now existing shall think proper to admit, shall not be prohibited by the Congress prior to the Year one thousand eight hundred and eight, but a Tax or duty may be imposed on such Importation, not exceeding ten dollars for each Person.

The Privilege of the Writ of Habeas Corpus shall not be suspended, unless when in Cases of Rebellion or Invasion the public Safety may require it.

No Bill of Attainder or ex post facto Law shall be passed.

[No Capitation, or other direct, Tax shall be laid, unless in Proportion to the Census or Enumeration herein before directed to be taken.]*

No Tax or Duty shall be laid on Articles exported from any State.

No Preference shall be given by any Regulation of Commerce or Revenue to the Ports of one State over those of another: nor shall Vessels bound to, or from, one State, be obliged to enter, clear, or pay Duties in another.

No Money shall be drawn from the Treasury, but in Consequence of Appropriations made by Law; and a regular Statement and Account of the Receipts and Expenditures of all public Money shall be published from time to time.

No Title of Nobility shall be granted by the United States: And no Person holding any Office of Profit or Trust under them, shall, without the Consent of the Congress, accept of any present, Emolument, Office, or Title, of any kind whatever, from any King, Prince, or foreign State.

SECTION. 10.

No State shall enter into any Treaty, Alliance, or Confederation; grant Letters of Marque and Reprisal; coin Money; emit Bills of Credit; make any Thing but gold and silver Coin a Tender in Payment of Debts; pass any Bill of Attainder, ex post facto Law, or Law impairing the Obligation of Contracts, or grant any Title of Nobility.

No State shall, without the Consent of the Congress, lay any Imposts or Duties on Imports or Exports, except what may be absolutely necessary for executing it's inspection Laws: and the net Produce of all Duties and Imposts, laid by any State on Imports or Exports, shall be for the Use of the Treasury of the United States; and all such Laws shall be subject to the Revision and Controul of the Congress.

No State shall, without the Consent of Congress, lay any Duty of Tonnage, keep Troops, or Ships of War in time of Peace, enter into any Agreement or Compact with another State, or with a foreign Power, or engage in War, unless actually invaded, or in such imminent Danger as will not admit of delay.

SECTION. 1.

The executive Power shall be vested in a President of the United States of America. He shall hold his Office during the Term of four Years, and, together with the Vice President, chosen for the same Term, be elected, as follows:

Each State shall appoint, in such Manner as the Legislature thereof may direct, a Number of Electors, equal to the whole Number of Senators and Representatives to which the State may be entitled in the Congress: but no Senator or Representative, or Person holding an Office of Trust or Profit under the United States, shall be appointed an Elector.

[The Electors shall meet in their respective States, and vote by Ballot for two Persons, of whom one at least shall not be an Inhabitant of the same State with themselves. And they shall make a List of all the Persons voted for, and of the Number of Votes for each; which List they shall sign and certify, and transmit sealed to the Seat of the Government of the United States, directed to the President of the Senate. The President of the Senate shall, in the Presence of the Senate and House of Representatives, open all the Certificates, and the Votes shall then be counted. The Person having the greatest Number of Votes shall be the President, if such Number be a Majority of the whole Number of Electors appointed; and if there be more than one who have such Majority, and have an equal Number of Votes, then the House of Representatives shall immediately chuse by Ballot one of them for President; and if no Person have a Majority, then from the five highest on the List

the said House shall in like Manner chuse the President. But in chusing the President, the Votes shall be taken by States, the Representation from each State having one Vote; A quorum for this Purpose shall consist of a Member or Members from two thirds of the States, and a Majority of all the States shall be necessary to a Choice. In every Case, after the Choice of the President, the Person having the greatest Number of Votes of the Electors shall be the Vice President. But if there should remain two or more who have equal Votes, the Senate shall chuse from them by Bal- lot the Vice

President.]*

The Congress may determine the Time of chusing the Electors, and the Day on which they shall give their Votes; which Day shall be the same throughout the United States.

No Person except a natural born Citizen, or a Citizen of the United States, at the time of the Adoption of this Constitution, shall be eligible to the Office of President; neither shall any person be eligible to that Office who shall not have attained to the Age of thirty five Years, and been fourteen Years a Resident within the United States.

[In Case of the Removal of the President from Office, or of his Death, Resignation, or Inability to discharge the Powers and Duties of the said Office, the Same shall devolve on the Vice President, and the Congress may by Law provide for the Case of Removal, Death, Resignation or Inability, both of the President and Vice President, declaring what Officer shall then act as President, and such Officer shall act accordingly, until the Disability be removed, or a President shall be elected.]*

The President shall, at stated Times, receive for his Services, a Compensation, which shall neither be increased nor diminished during the Period for which he shall have been elected, and he shall not receive within that Period any other Emolument from the United States, or any of them.

Before he enter on the Execution of his Office, he shall take the following Oath or Affirmation:- "I do solemnly swear (or affirm) that I will faithfully execute the Office of President of the United States, and will to the best of my Ability, preserve, protect and defend the Constitution of the United States."

SECTION. 2.

The President shall be Commander in Chief of the Army and Navy of the United States, and of the Militia of the several States, when called into the actual Service of the United States; he may require the Opinion, in writing, of the principal Officer in each of the executive Departments, upon any Subject relating to the Duties of their respective Offices, and he shall have Power to grant Reprieves and Pardons for Offenses against the United States, except in Cases of Impeachment.

He shall have Power, by and with the Advice and Consent of the Senate, to make Treaties, provided two thirds of the Senators present concur; and he shall nominate, and by and with the Advice and Consent of the Senate, shall appoint Ambassadors, other public Ministers and Consuls, Judges of the supreme Court, and all other Officers of the United States, whose Appointments are not herein otherwise provided for, and which shall be established by Law: but the Congress may by Law vest the Appointment of such inferior Officers, as they think proper, in the President alone, in the Courts of Law, or in the Heads of Departments.

The President shall have Power to fill up all Vacancies that may happen during the Recess of the Senate, by granting Commissions which shall expire at the End of their next Session.

SECTION. 3.

He shall from time to time give to the Congress Information of the State of the Union, and recommend to their Consideration such Measures as he shall judge necessary and expedient; he may, on extraordinary Occasions, convene both Houses, or either of them, and in Case of Disagreement between them, with Respect to the Time of Adjournment, he may adjourn them to such Time as he shall think proper; he shall receive Ambassadors and other public Ministers; he shall take Care that the Laws be faith- fully executed, and shall Commission all the Officers of the United States.

SECTION. 4.

The President, Vice President and all civil Officers of the United States, shall be removed from Office on Impeachment for, and Conviction of, Treason, Bribery, or other high Crimes and Misdemeanors.

Article III

SECTION. 1.

The judicial Power of the United States, shall be vested in one supreme Court, and in such inferior Courts as the Congress may from time to time ordain and establish. The Judges, both of the supreme and inferior Courts, shall hold their Offices during good Behaviour, and shall at stated Times, receive for their Services, a Compensation, which shall not be diminished during their Continuance in Office.

SECTION. 2.

The judicial Power shall extend to all Cases, in Law and Equity, arising under this Constitution, the Laws of the United States, and Treaties made, or which shall be made, under their Authority; to all Cases affecting Ambassadors, other public Ministers and Consuls; - to all Cases of admiralty and maritime Jurisdiction; to Controversies to which the United States shall be a Party; to Controversies between two or more States; [between a State and Citizens of another State;-]* between Citizens of different States, between Citizens of the same State claiming Lands under Grants of different States, [and between a State, or the Citizens thereof;- and foreign States, Citizens or Subjects.]*

In all Cases affecting Ambassadors, other public Ministers and Consuls, and those in which a State shall be Party, the supreme Court shall have original Jurisdiction. In all the other Cases before mentioned, the supreme Court shall have appellate Jurisdiction, both as to Law and Fact, with such Exceptions, and under such Regulations as the Congress shall make.

The Trial of all Crimes, except in Cases of Impeachment; shall be by Jury; and such Trial shall be held in the State where the said Crimes shall have been committed; but when not committed within any State, the Trial shall be at such Place or Places as the Congress may by Law have directed.

SECTION. 3.

Treason against the United States, shall consist only in levying War against them, or in adhering to their Enemies, giving them Aid and Comfort. No Person shall be convicted of Treason unless on the Testimony of two Witnesses to the same overt Act, or on Confession in open Court.

The Congress shall have Power to declare the Punishment of

Treason, but no Attainder of Treason shall work Corruption of Blood, or Forfeiture except during the Life of the Person attainted.

Article IV

SECTION. 1.

Full Faith and Credit shall be given in each State to the public Acts, Records, and judicial Proceedings of every other State. And the Congress may by general Laws prescribe the Manner in which such Acts, Records and Proceedings shall be proved, and the Effect thereof.

SECTION. 2.

The Citizens of each State shall be entitled to all Privileges and Immunities of Citizens in the several States.
A Person charged in any State with Treason, Felony, or other Crime, who shall flee from Justice, and be found in another State, shall on Demand of the executive Authority of the State from which he fled, be delivered up, to be removed to the State having Jurisdiction of the Crime.

[No Person held to Service or Labour in one State, under the Laws thereof, escaping into another, shall, in Consequence of any Law or Regulation therein, be discharged from such Service or Labour, but shall be delivered up on Claim of the Party to whom such Service or Labour may be due.]*

SECTION. 3.

New States may be admitted by the Congress into this Union; but no new State shall be formed or erected within the Jurisdiction of any other State; nor any State be formed by the Junction of two or more States, or Parts of States, without the Consent of the Legislatures of the States concerned as well as of the Congress.

The Congress shall have Power to dispose of and make all needful Rules and Regulations respecting the Territory or other Property belonging to the United States; and nothing in this Constitution shall be so construed as to Prejudice any Claims of the United States, or of any particular State.

SECTION. 4.

The United States shall guarantee to every State in this Union a Republican Form of Government, and shall protect each of them against Invasion; and on Application of the Legislature, or of the Executive (when the Legislature cannot be convened) against domestic Violence.

Article V

The Congress, whenever two thirds of both Houses shall deem it necessary, shall propose Amendments to this Constitution, or, on the Application of the Legislatures of two thirds of the several States, shall call a Convention for pro- posing Amendments, which in either Case, shall be valid to all Intents and Purposes, as Part of this Constitution, when ratified by the Legislatures of three-fourths of the several States, or by Conventions in three fourths thereof, as the one or the other Mode of Ratification may be proposed by the Congress; Provided that no Amendment which may be made prior to the Year One thousand eight hundred and eight shall in any Manner affect the first and fourth Clauses in the Ninth Section of the first Article; and that no State, without its Consent, shall be deprived of its equal Suffrage in the Senate.

Article VI

All Debts contracted and Engagements entered into, before the Adoption of this Constitution, shall be as valid against the United States under this Constitution, as under the Confederation.

This Constitution, and the Laws of the United States which shall be made in Pursuance thereof; and all Treaties made, or which shall be made, under the Authority of the United States, shall be the supreme Law of the Land; and the Judges in every State shall be bound thereby, any Thing in the Constitution or Laws of any State to the Contrary notwithstanding.

The Senators and Representatives before mentioned, and the Members of the several State Legislatures, and all executive and judicial Officers, both of the United States and of the several States, shall be bound by Oath or Affirmation, to support this Constitution; but no religious Test shall ever be required as a Qualification to any

Office or public Trust under the United States.

The Ratification of the Conventions of nine States, shall be sufficient for the Establishment of this Constitution between the States so ratifying the Same.

Done in Convention by the Unanimous Consent of the States present the Seventeenth Day of September in the Year of our Lord one thousand seven hundred and Eighty seven and of the Independence of the United States of America the Twelfth In Witness whereof We have hereunto subscribed our Names,

Go. Washington--Presidt: and deputy from Virginia

NEW HAMPSHIRE

John Langdon Nicholas Gilman

MASSACHUSETTS

Nathaniel Gorham Rufus King

CONNECTICUT

Wm. Saml. Johnson Roger Sherman

NEW YORK

Alexander Hamilton

NEW JERSEY

Wil: Livingston David Brearley Wm. Paterson Jona: Dayton

PENNSYLVANIA

B Franklin Thomas Mifflin Robt Morris Geo. Clymer Thos. FitzSimons Jared Ingersoll James Wilson Gouv Morris

CONSTITUTION OF THE UNITED STATES

DELAWARE

Geo: Read

Gunning Bedford jun John Dickinson Richard Bassett
Jaco: Broom

MARYLAND

James McHenry
Dan of St. Thos. Jenifer Danl Carroll

VIRGINIA

John Blair-
James Madison Jr.

NORTH CAROLINA

Wm. Blount
Richd. Dobbs Spaight Hu Williamson

SOUTH CAROLINA

J. Rutledge
Charles Cotesworth Pinckney Charles Pinckney
Pierce Butler

GEORGIA

William Few Abr Baldwin

Attest William Jackson Secretary

In Convention Monday September 17th, 1787. Present
The States of

New Hampshire, Massachusetts, Connecticut, Mr. Hamilton
from New York, New Jersey, Pennsylvania, Delaware, Maryland,
Virginia, North Carolina, South Carolina and Georgia.

Resolved,
That the preceeding Constitution be laid before the United States in
Congress assembled, and that it is the Opinion
of this Convention, that it should afterwards be submitted to
a Convention of Delegates, chosen in each State by the People
thereof, under the Recommendation of its Legislature, for their
Assent and Ratification; and that each Convention assenting to,

and ratifying the Same, should give Notice thereof to the United States in Congress assembled. Resolved, That it is the Opinion of this Convention, that as soon as the Conventions of nine States shall have ratified this Constitution, the United States in Congress assembled should fix a Day on which Electors should be appointed by the States which shall have ratified the same, and a Day on which the Electors should assemble to vote for the President, and the Time and Place for commencing Proceedings under this Constitution.

That after such Publication the Electors should be appointed, and the Senators and Representatives elected: That the Electors should meet on the Day fixed for the Election of the President, and should transmit their Votes certified, signed, sealed and directed, as the Constitution requires, to the Secretary of the United States in Congress assembled, that the Senators and Representatives should convene at the Time and Place assigned; that the Senators should appoint a President of the Senate, for the sole Purpose of receiving, opening and counting the Votes for President; and, that after he shall be chosen, the Congress, together with the President, should, without Delay, proceed to execute this Constitution.

By the unanimous Order of the Convention

Go. Washington-Presidt: W. JACKSON Secretary.

"Shhhh...these are the unspoken today it seems, but these are a list of your rights by God, not man, nor any government. You must understand that the second amendment has to be your most guarded, why? Because if they (the government) succeed in regulating or taking this amendment away from you, all your other rights listed here will fall victim to easy elimination, and you cannot afford to let that happen to your children and your children's offspring. You cannot be the generation to allow this to be taken from your people. Read, Study, and Know your rights, then USE them..."

THE AMENDMENTS TO THE CONSTITUTION OF THE UNITED STATES AS RATIFIED BY THE STATES

Preamble to the Bill of Rights

Congress of the United States
begun and held at the City of New-York, on Wednesday the fourth of March,
one thousand seven hundred and eighty nine

THE Conventions of a number of the States, having at the time of their adopting the Constitution, expressed a desire, in order to prevent misconstruction or abuse of its powers, that further declaratory and restrictive clauses should be added: And as extending the ground of public confidence in the Government, will best ensure the beneficent ends of its institution.

RESOLVED by the Senate and House of Representatives of the United States of America,
in Congress assembled, two thirds of both Houses concurring, that the following Articles be proposed to the Legislatures of the several States, as amendments
to the Constitution of the United States, all, or any of which Articles, when ratified by three fourths of the said Legislatures, to be valid to all intents and purposes, as part of the said Constitution; viz.

ARTICLES in addition to, and Amendment of the Constitution of the United States of America, proposed by Congress, and ratified by the Legislatures of the several States, pursuant to the fifth Article of the original Constitution.

(Note: The first 10 amendments to the Constitution were ratified December 15, 1791, and form what is known as the "Bill of Rights.")

Amendment I.

Congress shall make no law respecting an establishment of religion, or prohibiting the free exercise thereof; or abridging the freedom of speech, or of the press, or the right of the people peaceably to assemble, and to petition the Government for a redress of grievances.

Amendment II.

A well regulated Militia, being necessary to the security of a free State, the right of the people to keep and bear Arms, shall not be infringed.

Amendment III.

No Soldier shall, in time of peace be quartered in any house, without the consent of the Owner, nor in time of war, but in a manner to be prescribed by law.

Amendment IV.

The right of the people to be secure in their persons, houses, papers, and effects, against unreasonable searches and seizures, shall not be violated, and no Warrants shall issue, but upon probable cause, supported by Oath or affirmation, and particularly describing the place to be searched, and the persons or things to be seized.

Amendment V.

No person shall be held to answer for a capital, or otherwise infamous crime, unless on a presentment or indictment of a Grand Jury, except in cases arising in the land or naval forces, or in the Militia, when in actual service in time of War or public danger; nor shall any person be subject for the same offence to be twice put in jeopardy of life or limb; nor shall be compelled in any criminal case to be a witness against himself, nor be deprived of life, liberty, or property, without due process of law; nor shall private property be taken for public use, without just compensation.

Amendment VI.

In all criminal prosecutions, the accused shall enjoy the right to a speedy and public trial, by an impartial jury of the State and district wherein the crime shall have been committed, which district shall have been previously ascertained by law, and to be informed of the nature and cause of the accusation; to be confronted with the witnesses against him; to have compulsory process for obtaining wit- nesses in his favor, and to have the Assistance of Counsel for his defence.

Amendment VII.

In suits at common law, where the value in controversy shall exceed twenty dollars, the right of trial by jury shall be preserved, and no fact tried by a jury shall be otherwise re- examined in any Court of the United States, than according to the rules of the common law.

Amendment VIII.

Excessive bail shall not be required, nor excessive fines imposed, nor cruel and unusual punishments inflicted.

Amendment IX.

The enumeration in the Constitution, of certain rights, shall not be construed to deny or disparage others retained by the people.

Amendment X.

The powers not delegated to the United States by the Constitution, nor prohibited by it to the States, are reserved to the States respectively, or to the people.

Amendment XI.

Passed by Congress March 4, 1794. Ratified February 7, 1795.

(Note: A portion of Article III, Section 2 of the Constitution was modified by the 11th Amendment.)

The Judicial power of the United States shall not be construed to extend to any suit in law or equity, commenced or prosecuted against one of the United States by Citizens of another State, or by Citizens or Subjects of any Foreign State.

Amendment XII.

Passed by Congress December 9, 1803. Ratified June 15, 1804.

(Note: A portion of Article II, Section 1 of the Constitution was changed by the 12th Amendment.)

The Electors shall meet in their respective states, and vote by ballot for President and Vice-President, one of whom, at least, shall not be an inhabitant of the same state with themselves; they shall name in their ballots the person voted for as President, and in distinct ballots the person voted

for as Vice-President, and they shall make distinct lists of all persons voted for as President, and of all persons voted for as Vice-President, and of the number of votes for each, which lists

they shall sign and certify, and transmit sealed
to the seat of the government of the United States, directed to the
President of the Senate;-the President of the Senate shall, in the
presence of the Senate and House of Representatives, open all the
certificates and the votes shall then be counted;-The person having
the greatest number of votes for President, shall be the President,
if such number be a majority of the whole number of Electors
appointed; and if no person have such majority, then from the
persons having the highest numbers not exceeding three on the
list of those voted for as President, the House of Representatives
shall choose immediately, by ballot, the President. But in choosing
the President, the votes shall be taken by states, the representation
from each state having one vote; a quorum for this purpose shall
consist of a member or members from two-thirds of the states, and
a majority of all the states shall be necessary to a choice. [And if the
House of Representatives shall not choose a President whenever
the right of choice shall devolve upon them, before the fourth
day of March next following, then the Vice-President shall act as
President, as in case of the death or other constitutional disability
of the President.-]* The person having the greatest number of votes
as Vice-President, shall be the Vice-President, if such number be a
majority of the whole number

of Electors appointed, and if no person have a majority, then from
the two highest numbers on the list, the Senate shall choose the
Vice-President; a quorum for the purpose shall consist of two-
thirds of the whole number of Senators, and a majority of the whole
number shall be necessary to

a choice. But no person constitutionally ineligible to the office of
President shall be eligible to that of Vice-President of the United
States.

*Superseded by Section 3 of the 20th Amendment.

Amendment XIII.

Passed by Congress January 31, 1865. Ratified December 6, 1865.

*(Note: A portion of Article IV, Section 2 of the Constitution was changed
by the 13th Amendment.)*

SECTION 1.

Neither slavery nor involuntary servitude, except as a punishment for crime whereof the party shall have been duly convicted, shall exist within the United States, or any place subject to their jurisdiction.

SECTION 2.

Congress shall have power to enforce this article by appropriate legislation.

Amendment XIV.

Passed by Congress June 13, 1866. Ratified July 9, 1868.

(Note: Article I, Section 2 of the Constitution was modified by Section 2 of the 14th Amendment.)

SECTION 1.

All persons born or naturalized in the United States and subject to the jurisdiction thereof, are citizens of the United States and of the State wherein they reside. No State shall make or enforce any law which shall abridge the privileges or immunities of citizens of the United States; nor shall

any State deprive any person of life, liberty, or property, without due process of law; nor deny to any person within its jurisdiction the equal protection of the laws.

SECTION 2.

Representatives shall be apportioned among the several States according to their respective numbers, counting the whole number of persons in each State, excluding Indians not taxed. But when the right to vote at any election for the choice of electors for President and Vice President of the United States, Representatives in Congress, the Executive and Judicial officers of a State, or the members of the Legislature thereof, is denied to any of the male inhabit- ants of such State, [being twenty-one years of age,]* and citizens of the United States, or in any way abridged, except for participation in rebellion, or other crime, the basis of representation therein shall be reduced in the proportion which the number of such male citizens shall bear to the whole number of male citizens twenty-one years of age in such State.

SECTION 3.

No person shall be a Senator or Representative in Congress, or elector of President and Vice President, or hold any office, civil or military, under the United States, or under any State, who, having previously taken an oath, as a member of Congress, or as an officer of the United States, or as a member of any State legislature, or as an executive or judicial officer of any State, to support the Constitution of the United States, shall have engaged in insurrection or rebellion against the same, or given aid or comfort to the enemies thereof. But Congress may by a vote of two-thirds of each House, remove such disability.

SECTION 4.

The validity of the public debt of the United States, authorized by law, including debts incurred for payment of pensions and bounties for services in suppressing insurrection or rebellion, shall not be questioned. But neither the United States nor any State shall assume or pay any debt
or obligation incurred in aid of insurrection or rebellion against the United States, or any claim for the loss or emancipation of any slave; but all such debts, obligations and claims shall be held illegal and void.

SECTION 5.

The Congress shall have the power to enforce, by appropriate legislation, the provisions of this article.

*Changed by Section 1 of the 26th Amendment.

Amendment XV.

Passed by Congress February 26, 1869. Ratified February 3, 1870.

SECTION 1.

The right of citizens of the United States to vote shall not be denied or abridged by the United States or by any State on account of race, color, or previous condition of servitude.

SECTION 2.

The Congress shall have the power to enforce this article by appropriate legislation.

Amendment XVI.

Passed by Congress July 2, 1909. Ratified February 3, 1913.

(Note: Article I, Section 9 of the Constitution was modified by the 16th Amendment.)

The Congress shall have power to lay and collect taxes on incomes, from whatever source derived, without apportionment among the several States, and without regard to any census or enumeration.

Amendment XVII.

Passed by Congress May 13, 1912. Ratified April 8, 1913.

(Note: Article I, Section 3 of the Constitution was modified by the 17th Amendment.)

The Senate of the United States shall be composed of two Senators from each State, elected by the people thereof, for six years; and each Senator shall have one vote. The electors in each State shall have the qualifications requisite for electors of the most numerous branch of the State legislatures.

When vacancies happen in the representation of any State in the Senate, the executive authority of such State shall issue writs of election to fill such vacancies: Provided, That the legislature of any State may empower the executive thereof to make temporary appointments until the people fill the vacancies by election as the legislature may direct.

This amendment shall not be so construed as to affect the election or term of any Senator chosen before it becomes valid as part of the Constitution.

Amendment XVIII.

Passed by Congress December 18, 1917. Ratified January 16, 1919. Repealed by the 21st Amendment, December 5, 1933.

SECTION 1.

After one year from the ratification of this article the manufacture, sale, or transportation of intoxicating liquors within, the importation thereof into, or the exportation thereof from the United States and all territory subject to the jurisdiction thereof for beverage purposes is hereby prohibited.

SECTION 2.

The Congress and the several States shall have concurrent power to enforce this article by appropriate legislation.

SECTION 3.

This article shall be inoperative unless it shall have been ratified as an amendment to the Constitution by the legislatures of the several States, as provided in the Constitution, within seven years from the date of the submission hereof to the States by the Congress.

Amendment XIX.

Passed by Congress June 4, 1919. Ratified August 18, 1920.

The right of citizens of the United States to vote shall not be denied or abridged by the United States or by any State on account of sex.

Congress shall have power to enforce this article by appropriate legislation.

Amendment XX.

Passed by Congress March 2, 1932. Ratified January 23, 1933.

(Note: Article I, Section 4 of the Constitution was modified by Section 2 of this Amendment. In addition, a portion of the 12th Amendment was superseded by Section 3.)

SECTION 1.

The terms of the President and the Vice President shall end at noon on the 20th day of January, and the terms of Senators and Representatives at noon on the 3d day of January, of the years in which such terms would have ended if this article had not been ratified; and the terms of their successors shall then begin.

SECTION 2.

The Congress shall assemble at least once in every year, and such meeting shall begin at noon on the 3d day of January, unless they shall by law appoint a different day.

SECTION 3.

If, at the time fixed for the beginning of the term of the President, the President elect shall have died, the Vice President elect shall become President. If a President shall not have been chosen before the time fixed for the beginning of his term, or if the President elect shall have failed to qualify, then the Vice President elect shall act as President until a President shall have qualified; and the Congress may by law provide for the case wherein neither a President elect nor a Vice President shall have qualified, declaring who shall then act as President, or the manner in which one who is to act shall be selected, and such person shall act accordingly until a President or Vice President shall have qualified.

SECTION 4.

The Congress may by law provide for the case of the death of any of the persons from whom the House of Representatives may choose a President whenever the right of choice shall have devolved upon them, and for the case of the death of any of the persons from whom the Senate may choose a Vice President whenever the right of choice shall have devolved upon them.

SECTION 5.

Sections 1 and 2 shall take effect on the 15th day of October following the ratification of this article.

SECTION 6.

This article shall be inoperative unless it shall have been ratified as an amendment to the Constitution by the legislatures of three-fourths of the several States within seven years from the date of its submission.

Amendment XXI.

Passed by Congress February 20, 1933. Ratified December 5, 1933.

SECTION 1.

The eighteenth article of amendment to the Constitution of the United States is hereby repealed.

SECTION 2.

The transportation or importation into any State, Territory, or possession of the United States for delivery or use therein of intoxicating liquors, in violation of the laws thereof, is hereby prohibited.

SECTION 3.

This article shall be inoperative unless it shall have been ratified as an amendment to the Constitution by conventions in the several States, as provided in the Constitution, within seven years from the date of the submission hereof to the States by the Congress.

Amendment XXII.

Passed by Congress March 21, 1947. Ratified February 27, 1951.

SECTION 1.

No person shall be elected to the office of the President more than twice, and no person who has held the office of President, or acted as President, for more than two years of a term to which some other person was elected President shall be elected to the office of President more than once. But this Article shall not apply to any person holding the office of President when this Article was proposed by Congress, and shall not prevent any person who may be holding the office of President, or acting as President, during the term within which this Article becomes operative from holding the office of President or acting as President during the remainder of such term.

SECTION 2.

This article shall be inoperative unless it shall have been ratified as an amendment to the Constitution by the legislatures of three-fourths of the several States within seven years from the date of its submission to the States by the Congress.

Amendment XXIII.

Passed by Congress June 16, 1960. Ratified March 29, 1961.

SECTION 1.

The District constituting the seat of Government of the United States shall appoint in such manner as Congress may direct:

A number of electors of President and Vice President equal to the whole number of Senators and Representatives
in Congress to which the District would be entitled if it were a State, but in no event more than the least populous State; they shall be in addition to those appointed by the States, but they shall be considered, for the purposes of

the election of President and Vice President, to be electors appointed by a State; and they shall meet in the District and perform such duties as provided by the twelfth article of amendment.

SECTION 2.

The Congress shall have power to enforce this article by appropriate legislation.

Amendment XXIV.

Passed by Congress August 27, 1962. Ratified January 23, 1964.

SECTION 1.

The right of citizens of the United States to vote in any primary or other election for President or Vice President, for electors for President or Vice President, or for Senator or Representative in Congress, shall not be denied or abridged by the United States or any State by reason of failure to pay poll tax or other tax.

SECTION 2.

The Congress shall have power to enforce this article by appropriate legislation.

Amendment XXV.

Passed by Congress July 6, 1965. Ratified February 10, 1967.

(Note: Article II, Section 1 of the Constitution was modified by the 25th Amendment.)

SECTION 1.

In case of the removal of the President from office or of his death or resignation, the Vice President shall become President.

SECTION 2.

Whenever there is a vacancy in the office of the Vice President, the President shall nominate a Vice President who shall take office upon confirmation by a majority vote of both Houses of Congress.

SECTION 3.

Whenever the President transmits to the President pro tempore of the Senate and the Speaker of the House of Representatives his written declaration that he is unable to discharge the powers and duties of his office, and until he transmits to them a written declaration to the contrary, such powers and duties shall be discharged by the Vice President as Acting President.

SECTION 4.

Whenever the Vice President and a majority of either the principal officers of the executive departments or of such other body as Congress may by law provide, transmit to the President pro tempore of the Senate and the Speaker of the House of Representatives their written declaration that the President is unable to discharge the powers and duties of his office, the Vice President shall immediately assume the powers and duties of the office as Acting President.

Thereafter, when the President transmits to the President

pro tempore of the Senate and the Speaker of the House of Representatives his written declaration that no inability exists, he shall resume the powers and duties of his office un- less the Vice President and a majority of either the principal officers of the executive department or of such other body as Congress may by law provide, transmit within four days to the President pro tempore of the Senate and the Speaker of the House of Representatives their written declaration that the President is unable to discharge the powers and duties of his office. Thereupon Congress shall decide the issue, assembling within forty-eight hours for that purpose if not in session. If the Congress, within twenty-one days after receipt of the latter written declaration, or, if Congress is not in session, within twenty-one days after Congress is required to assemble, determines by two-thirds vote of both Houses that the President is unable to discharge the powers and duties of his office, the Vice President shall continue to discharge the same as Acting President; otherwise, the President shall resume the powers and duties of his office.

Amendment XXVI.

Passed by Congress March 23, 1971. Ratified July 1, 1971.

(Note: Amendment 14, Section 2 of the Constitution was modified by Section 1 of the 26th Amendment.)

SECTION 1.

The right of citizens of the United States, who are eighteen years of age or older, to vote shall not be denied or abridged by the United States or by any State on account of age.

SECTION 2.

The Congress shall have power to enforce this article by appropriate legislation.

Amendment XXVII.

Originally proposed Sept. 25, 1789. Ratified May 7, 1992.

No law, varying the compensation for the services of the Senators and Representatives, shall take effect, until an election of representatives shall have intervened.

"Now as there are only 27 amendments to the Constitution of the United States thus far, and not very many needs of additions to be added, one area that has very much became a necessity, is that those placed in positions of authority shall not be above any laws that the citizenship themselves have to be subject to, so much consideration must be paid upon the current <u>proposed</u> 28th amendment."

Proposed 28th Amendment: "Congress shall make and pass no law that exempts the Members of the United States Senate and the Members of the United Sates House of Representatives from any and all laws that the two Chambers of Congress pass that apply to the Citizens of the United States and the District of Columbia." (the District of Columbia is separate from the United States.) Congress shall make no rules in the United States Senate and the United States House of Representatives that give Members of both Chambers of Congress greater Medical, Educational, Financial Benefits or unfair advantage over other Federal, State, Municipal Employees or Employees in the Private Sector of the United States or the District of Columbia. While in the service of their office or in their retirement benefits plan. Any Senate Rules or House of Representative Rules that currently apply to, and are made by the United States Senate and the United States House of Representatives that unfairly put the aforementioned Members of the two Chambers of Congress above other Federal, State, Municipal or Private Sector Employees... in the law or in equity and that are contrary to the letter and spirit of our United States Constitution shall be abolished. "

"Now that you have a foundation to build upon, then build. Every citizen grows in effectiveness and strength as you increase your communications and networking. This guide gives you the actions you must take to achieve and maintain your authority within our Republic. Through these best practices and solutions we the people will increase the quality of your personal relationship with your network, within your local community, your county, your state, and your nation. The stronger your communication network, the more impact you will have in return. Communication is the strongest cornerstone you possess. Look, this guide is not an exhaustive list of tips and suggestions, we know the more avenues and conduits of communication you and your tribe uses, the greater your impact in accomplishing your mission."

A GUIDE TO COMMUNICATIONS AND NETWORKING

Word of Mouth Communication Technique

The purpose of the Word of Mouth Communication Technique is to have the ability to develop, maintain, and implement a local, statewide, and national network of communication that will prove effective even after modern technology, such as phone or email, is no longer available. This is a very strong possibility in some natural disasters, as well as, an attack on our grid system by an EMP (Electro Magnetic Pulse).

This technique (Word of Mouth Communication) is a foundational network that also acts as a knowledge builder, team builder, resource finder, member recruiter, and movement strengthener. It also helps identify the whereabouts of like-minded citizens, and activists and the groups of which they belong.

There are five phases to the Word of Mouth Communication Technique:

Phase One – Local Group Membership Networking

Best practice is to first start with your local area and/or group membership. The focus here, at this first level, when using the word of mouth communication technique (WOMT), is the encouragement of *each member* to organize their *own personal level network* to a point where they can then begin to communicate, educate, and recruit new and close surrounding candidates to join the local group (which is also joining the overall movement). This first phase (Personal Black Book) is the cornerstone that will begin to build a network that will reach out to, and tie in, the entire neighborhood, city, county, state, and eventually the country.

- Encourage each member to record all contacts into categories such as: group members, work colleagues, neighbors, family, and casual/acquaintances. Use name, address, phone

51

number, email, and notes, as basic contact information sought. The individual and personal network kept by each member allows full strength and effectiveness in communication to your group as a whole; the power of word and contacts as a key weapon to victory.

- Challenge each member to begin to build their personal networks and keep a record of them each month.
    o Build by initiating and approaching the people in your categories (one on one) and get to know them. Who they are, what they do, "get to know each other" type of discussions.
    o Categories identified such as Mayor, City Counsel, School Board, City Utilities, Chief of Police/Officers, County Sheriff/Deputies, Neighbors, Family, Veteran Groups, Business Leaders/Owners, etc.
    o Build by discussing issues of the day with the people in your categories to share, educate, influence, and mentor each other.
    o Build by inviting them to your meetings and telling them that engaging and meeting with like-minded patriots is vital to gaining back and maintaining our Republic and to save our liberties and freedoms that our forefathers and veterans have bled, sacrificed and died for, over the past two centuries.
    o Build by using modern technologies (while they are useful) to reach out to all your categories as initiating some face-to-face contacts.
    o Build by visiting your contacts in their homes, place of work, meetings, and places of mutual settings.
    o Build by taking notes on skills, assets, and resources each person may have. Practice this note taking, as it will prove to be a priceless resource in future planning and organizing.
    o DO NOT EVER TAKE A LIST FROM SOMEONE ELSE WITHOUT CONNECTING WITH EACH CONTACT FOR YOURSELF. YOUR NETWORK IS JUST THAT, YOURS. You will only benefit from this type of network building and gain trust and credibility by not giving your list to others without permission. As you make your list get said permission first from each to share with group or others. Then mark such permissions onto your list where you can

keep your lists separate.

- o Share the network information with a master list (with permission of each contact) to the group. List each category of contact information to include the "notes" column that lists assets to the movement for future planning if needed.

This level is complete when all members begin to implement it. It is a continuous mission, but you will begin to see a steady growth in membership, more activists at events, a larger force to disseminate your mission's message, and it will help build your own skill sets that will be an asset to your group's effectiveness.

Phase Two – Local, County, State, National Government Network

The focus during this phase is to begin to research and connect with your governments at every level, the local, county, state and national levels, to begin your personal skill building in communicating and engaging with elected officials while educating them on the role of their constituency as the authority of our Republic to begin to build the public servant roles in our self-governing Republic.

- *Encourage each member to record all contacts into categories such as; title of governing body, members of governing body and their contact info. Use name, address, phone number, email, and notes, as the basic contact information sought. This list begins to bring back to you, the people, the authority of a self-governed republic as it was initially entitled, through a communication network you can now use for input and accountability.*
- *Examples of local, county, state, and national governing bodies may include, but are not limited to, the following:*
  - o *School Boards*
  - o *City Council*
  - o *City Planning and Zoning Commission*
  - o *City Mayor*
  - o *City Police Department*
  - o *County Commission/Supervisors*
  - o *County Sheriff Office*
  - o *County Republican Committee*

- County Democratic Committee
- State Senators
- State Representatives
- State Central Committees
- Governors
- US Senators
- US Representatives
- President of the United States

- Encourage members to reach out one on one, to have face-to-face introductions with these servants of the people, and get to know them on a personal level. This process trains members in dealing their various members of governing bodies, and in doing so builds confidence in gaining back the peoples' authority within the governed.

Phase Three – Neighboring Group Network

The focus in this phase is to begin to reach out and network with like-minded groups in your city, county, neighboring counties, state, and across the nation. The leadership, or coordinators of the group, should express the importance to reach out to neighboring groups in your city, then your county, then your neighboring counties and continue to spread out further in the state after each connection is made. Be sure to express to the membership of your group that this network building process to neighboring groups accomplishes the same education/assessment on a group level as it did with the membership level. It builds teamwork, resource sharing, identification of like-minded activist groups, where they are located, and an understanding of the different mission statements as well as the similarities of each group under this single movement.

- Invite leadership, trainers, experts, etc. from each group you make contact with, to speak at your group meetings to introduce and share expertise and best practices. Members of your group will need to do the same for the groups you make contact with. This information should be noted on the summary of the group within your recordings. As contact with each group is made face to face, one more arm of communication is constructed.

- Share websites, calendars, emails of leadership/coordinators with one another so events, rallies, and current missions are communicated in order to maximize impact and efficiency when you need pressure and turnout for an issue. Numbers and quantity are always strength within the movement; more voices heard and bodies seen help create an accurate representation of the people within the district, and ultimately within the overall movement.
- Seek out all like-minded groups, do not leave out any group from being contacted from your area. Meet face-to-face, one on one, and get to know the other like-minded groups. If the group is not conservative or like-minded then practice going to them to speak what your group is about to give an accurate portrayal of the movement, instead of them getting it from lame stream media.
- Be sure to record the group's name, location address, contact information, and notes that contain mission and assets in the movement.

Phase Four – National Group Network

The focus within the fourth phase is a best practice to research all national conservative groups, assess their mission statements, focus of efforts, and resources they each have to feed the overall movement. Treat them as you do with your membership and your neighboring groups. Work with, and support, those areas that meet your mission statement in winning back our Republic. We must also understand that there is one movement of the people, one fight, and We the People, are one, (E Pluribus Unum (from the many one). This is key to winning back the Republic. If a group you assess mission and example does not unite with We The People first and foremost, then move on, do not network with them as the amount of entanglements of political parties are very hard to release from once connected. It is better to judge on the action vs mission of each group to see the true vision they push.

- Research the history, website, contact info, state structure, and persons involved. There are a lot of great constitutional focused groups out there that are well worth getting to know and use as resources.

Phase Five – Implementing Word of Mouth Technique

The action of the Word of Mouth Technique will, beyond your belief, prove to be so effective in accomplishing the goals of our movement. By now you have set in place a foundation of membership that understand their roles within your groups' mission statement, and you will have empowered authority back to the American people that your group has contact with.

"By exercising/engaging the Word of Mouth Technique, you will have learned how to:

- *perfect your network*
- *collaborate, communicate, and work as a team*
- *support, respect, and identify equal and common ground with governing bodies and other groups*
- *assess and vet all conservative and like-minded groups around you."*

In the end, the Word of Mouth Technique will have put in place a network of communication that can stand on its own **even without the use of modern technology.** Because you have met with your membership and neighbors and know who they are, where they are, and what assets they possess **(Phase One);** because you met with your local, county, and state governments and know who they are, where they are, and how they operate **(Phase two);** because you physically met with your neighboring groups in your surrounding areas and know who they are, where they are, what mission they have, and what assets they possess **(Phase Three;)** and because you have reached out to, and communicated with, the national groups you know what their mission is, who they are, and what resources they possess **(Phase Four).** you can reach out with messaging, that will trigger a domino effect and reach your entire state and potentially the entire nation just through word of mouth. Below is an example using the state of Iowa to show how this overlap of communication will work just by talking with your surrounding counties only, and how that single message can travel by all groups using the Word of Mouth Technique.

The first slide just shows 47 groups (there are 78 groups now identified in Iowa this slide was made when there were 47) in the counties. The second slide shows a colored line around each group that uses the Word of Mouth Technique in just the surrounding counties around each group. You can see how the overlap then starts to travel with the message across state. In a bigger picture that is not shown, you can imagine if all states use this how the word/message begins to make its way across the nation. Best-case scenario is that modern technology will always be available which only enhances the Word of Mouth Technique one hundred fold. Keep in mind that it needs to be in place **and practiced** to be a rapid communication tool that is highly needed in our movement. Stay engaged by implementing and teaching the Word of Mouth Technique.

Lyon   Osceola   Dickinson   Emmet   Winnebago   Worth   Mitchell   Howard
                                    Kossuth   Winneshiek
                                                                                              Allamakee
Sioux   O'Brien   Clay   Palo   Hancock   Cerro   Floyd   Chickasaw   44
                          Alto   Gordo
                   8   40   14   6

Plymouth   Cherokee   Buena   Pocahontas   Humboldt   Wright   Franklin   Butler   Bremer
                      Vista   Fayette   Clayton
           5   3   25   13   9

45 46
Woodbury   Ida   Sac   Calhoun   Webster   Hamilton   Hardin   Grundy   Black   Buchanan   Delaware   Dubuque
                                                                        Hawk
   23   36   39   1   2   12

Monona   Crawford   Carroll   Greene   Boone   Story   Marshall   Tama   Benton   20
                                                                                       19   Jones   Jackson
                    4   42   Linn
                                                 41   21   18   Clinton

                                                 24 26 27   17   Cedar
Harrison   Shelby   Audubon   Guthrie   Dallas   28 Polk 29   Jasper   Poweshiek   Iowa   Johnson   38
   15   30 33   16   Scott
   35   31 32   Muscatine   37

Pottawattamie   Cass   Adair   Madison   Warren   Marion   Mahaska   Keokuk   Washington
   34   Louisa

Mills   Montgomery   Adams   Union   Clarke   Lucas   Monroe   Wapello   Jefferson
   22   7   43   Henry   Des Moines
                                                                                      11

Fremont   Page   Taylor   Ringgold   Decatur   Wayne   Appanoose   Davis   Van Buren   47
                                        10   Lee

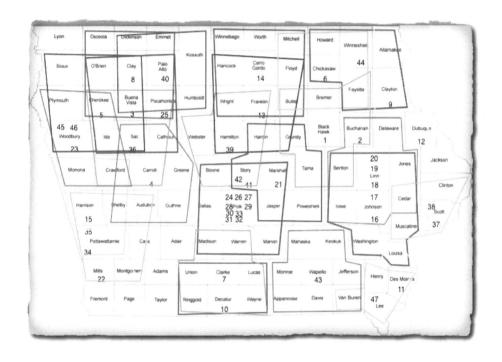

Other means of communication and their best practices:

- *News Papers*

  So believe it or not, newspapers still have a large audience especially in small town USA and in larger cities the online version of the same hard copy of the paper that is at your local newsstand. Although it is hard to get full blown articles put in your local papers, as you continue to reach out to others in your communities, the editor of your local paper would be an outstanding network partner for you and your group especially when pushing out a message or events. The letter to the editors are always a huge hit and smaller with letters range from 300 to 500 words. Do not overlook this opportunity as newspapers can be a very useful platform in getting the word out on a message your working on.

- *Phone*

Staying in communication via phone with each member in your   network around the state is extremely important. Individual phone calls can be time-consuming so having a schedule or rotation of phone calls that you stick to can be helpful. Sometimes individuals in your network will be more comfortable brainstorming, strategizing, or sharing important information with you on a one on one phone call, rather than they would in person or on a conference call with several people. However, this does not negate the importance of holding regular group size, statewide (or regional calls within your county or state) conference calls. These statewide calls can be highly effective for coordinating statewide efforts and sharing critical information.

Each state is different, you'll need to determine the schedule (weekly, bi-weekly, monthly, etc) that works best for the coordinators in your state. If you do not already have a conference call service you're using, you can sign up for a free accounts and conference call numbers through websites and even social media platforms.

You'll also need to determine who will host or MC the conference call. It's best to have two or three people that can host different parts of the call, that can rotate hosting the call, or can fill in if the scheduled host is unable to MC the last minute. Also, by having more than one host, it can help during the Q&A as you may have more than one person that has researched or studied the subject you're discussing on the call.

The host, or hosts, will also be responsible for setting up

the conference call itself, setting the agenda, and sending out reminders, with the agenda, to the other hosts and coordinators that are invited to attend the call. Having a general agenda template that you can re-use for each conference call is a great idea. This allows you to save time as you set the agenda for each call if you only have to insert the pertinent details, topics, and guests if applicable, rather than coming up with a brand new agenda from scratch each time. Be sure to confirm your host(s) and guest(s) prior to sending out the agenda to all your conference call attendees.

To help avoid the dreaded *"death by conference call"* always be mindful of the time. Once your conference call has started, we suggest a brief overview of the agenda, introduce the topics that will be discussed, and then have any guests go first. Five minutes, with a few minutes for Q&A is generally more than enough time for a guest speaker (be sure to let the speaker know at the time you book them that they will only have this amount of time so they can have their presentation or talking points ready to present in this amount of time). On a phone call attention rates begin to drop if one person, no matter how charismatic they are, talks over 5 minutes without other actions or voices being heard.

A few conference call tips to mention:
- Always schedule time for Q&A after the guest speaker.
- Include time in your agenda for general Q&A after each topic is discussed, or at the very end of the call which allows you to get through all topics prior to opening up for questions.
- Have a set of *"timing rules"* and *"call rules"* at the top of your agenda. By reminding all attendees of these rules at the top of each call it will help your conference calls stay on track and also be respectful of each attendee's time. Over time these reminders and rules should become second nature to all those involved with the calls.
- Always follow up with a conference call summary or a list of tasks/to-do's or action items that were from the outcome of

the call. Be sure to include the date and time of the next call in this summary.

- *Email*

  Developing and maintaining an email list based on your networking with all the people and groups in your state should be a top priority for Local and State leaders in any given state. One of the best ways to develop and maintain this list is by personally meeting with leaders face to face in your state. These meetings can provide a great networking opportunity where you can introduce yourself and your group, and exchange all necessary contact information that can be added to your ever evolving email list. Another method for building your list is by doing online research of all the groups in your state.

  As your network email list grows you can begin to categorize and organize the various types of contacts you may have on your list. For example: local groups, statewide groups, national groups, supporters, volunteers, supportive businesses, election officials, etc.
  A personal email list leads to knowledge of all you come in contact with and knowledge of resources and strengths out there, but most of all a personal email list becomes the veins and arteries of which all your efforts become engaging, and quickly unifying with your efforts. It truly elevates the "More heads are better than one" truth, as well as serves in a quick reaction tool in a very quick paced society.

  There are many free email providers to choose from. Always do your own research to determine which will work best for you, but some of the most popular are: Gmail from Google, Hotmail, and Yahoo. Another option for emailing your contacts is using a service such as Mailchimp. Mailchimp is free up to a certain number of contacts on your list, and how many emails you send per month. The benefit of using a service like Mailchimp is that it includes analytics so you can see the open rate of your email and who is opening your emails.

- *Social Media/Chat*

  Facebook and Twitter are two of the most popular and widely used social media platforms in the past. Many groups have used options available on Facebook instead of maintaining their own website. Groups can start a "page" that is visible and open to the public where they share news, events, and more, and there are "private groups" that groups can utilize. Private groups are not visible to the public, invitations must be sent to individuals in order to access and post on the page; this is a great option for real time internal communications.

  Social media is in fact a great tool to strengthen your numbers and impact in relation to messaging. We mentioned two above but there are so many and new ones come up all the time. The trick is to find the ones who do not censor and are bias against strong conservative, patriotic, voices like yours. Other sites to check into are MEWE, Parler, TikTok, Clapper, Telegram, Klips, Rumble, Triller, Youtube, Linkedin, Signal, Snapchat, Whatsup, and so many many more. There are even some new ones in development like Just The Tip and others using block chain technology to protect against corruption and even censorship.

  The key is to join a many different social media sites and exploit the unique strengths that each has to offer. But do not join so many that you cannot manage them all. If there are many maybe identify friends or partners to be on some that you are not so that you cast a larger net with the messages you want to project.

  A best practice we want to share here. We call it a *"wave based tsunami of messaging"* effect when pushing out messaging. It looks like the following:

      I.   Create the message in its entirety, with key points

and directives or specifics spelled out within the message.

II.   Make as many different versions of the same message to get different looks at it, such as memes, reports, summaries, blasts etc. One for each platform you want to utilize or one for each day of the week.

III.   Then say you chose three platforms to get this message out, Facebook, Tiktok, and Telegram. Then on a specific time of the day, and a specific date, you and all your group members blasts out on facebook memes of your message. Then three days later on that date at a specific time you all blast out a detailed report of your message all at the same time on Tiktok. Finally, anther three days later you all again blast out at this specific time and date a summary of your message on Telegram. With each blast you push out a pulse of the same information from different accounts on the same date on the same platform.

IV.   This will increase your eyes on target, and hit different demographics across the board.

- *Websites*

  It is imperative that if you make a website for your group that you keep it updated to keep people wanting to continue to visit it and get the messages you want to get out. Your own website can be one of the best ways to mass communicate with the entire grassroots network within your state, and communicate with the public. This website option takes a little more work because you'll need to have at least one person in place that can maintain this website (this can be someone you pay, a volunteer, or a combination of both).

  You also must have a way to get as well as transmit questions to the visitor on your website, as well as a way to help you identify the visitor if needed.

  There might be some very interesting patriot minded

websites out there already that you can use as a great resource to get the latest news, events, other resources, and information you or your group can grow from.

Look into as well state level websites that have and create accurate data you can use in the forms of numbers, costs, bills, laws, schooling etc. Identifying such websites in tandem of your mission will pay out huge dividends in knowledge and credibility.

There are many website companies that offer basis website themes and/or hosting packages at reasonable prices. GoDaddy has website building tools and packages. Another platform is Shopify, although they are primarily an e-commerce platform, they do offer a variety of free and low-cost themes that can be used for websites that are not operating as an e-commerce business. Or, if you're wanting to build your own website, Wordpress has hundreds of options, many of which are free.

- *Talk Radio*
  It is very important to develop a habit of calling into your local talk radio shows. When you regularly call into your local talk radio shows it helps project your message over a large area. Over time, as your relationship and trust with the local talk radio show hosts grows, the more information you may gain, or you may garner invitations to meet with them, or coordinate on issues.
- The best practice in using talk radio shows to your advantage is to always have ready a written form of your talking points of an issue, 1. Key points that make your issue so important for others to know, 2. And a list of contact information where others can get a hold of you. Finally, to have prepared 3. A complete mission statement in your own words that will catch the ears of listeners of the show.
- Then just listen to your favorite talk radio shows and when they begin to cover a topic that is related to your mission, by all means call in as soon as possible and state your perspectives and goals. This is free advertisement, free markets, and freedom of speech at its best.

- This process has proven and will prove to be a great benefit for not only you and the listener but for the radio shows as well, who are eager to hear from the communities in which they broadcast.
- Gregg Cummings became very close friends with Talk Radio Show Host Simon Conway from WHO Radio 1040AM which is Ronald Reagan's old radio show back in the 50s. He first came in contact with Simon during a Tea Party Rally in Des Moines Iowa, they introduced themselves and exchanged business cards. It wasn't long after that that they were having lunch together off and on and a good friendship developed. Now every memorial day, or veterans day or any issue dealing with the military or patriotic efforts Simon Conway often calls on Gregg to have on his show as a guest to discuss those issues and perspectives. These kinds of showings brings greater attendance to rallies that are shared and begins greater discussions from regular folks driving to and from work in the afternoons.
- Linda Dorr, from the Laguna Patriots, Laguna Beach, California said this about the power of talk radio;

"In the last 2016 Presidential election I made great progress on communicating through Talk Radio and why we needed to 'Clean the Swamp!" She continued saying; *"Voters tune in regularly to their favorite Talk Radio shows throughout their day. That's why it was important for me to identify the most popular local radio shows throughout the Swing States to make calls to those stations.*

Local radio stations are easier to get into their shows then the other media venues.
I was fortunate to have the ability to speak with key local Talk Radio host in the Key Swing States. In fact, one Ohio Talk Radio host made the comment he believed he now had a National Radio Show because of my frequent calls from California into his Ohio station."

- *Television News*

  IMPORTANT: The first thing you need to know about television news is in today's hi-tech age you need to treat everyday in public as a day on television news. Always be aware that everyone "is" a news program if they are carrying a phone, and everyone carries a phone.

- So *lets look at some basics of a successful news interview, please be cognizant of these basics in all other situations and scenarios dealing with the media.*
    I. *Know your mission statement always:* know how to do a 40min discussion on it, a 30min discussion on it, a 10 min discussion on it and what we call an elevator summary of it, 1 min. This is key, not only in accomplishing your mission overall, but to educate anyone in any scenario about your mission and why it is so important.
    II. *Optics are always huge in any news story or interview:* what is your environment, what is around you, and how are you dressed and or groomed? All of these are front burner questions to be answered when in a news story. If your doing an interview about freedom and your wearing a pro-socialism shirt your credibility just went down the toilet. Or if you are defending the flag while standing there holding a flag that is touching the ground your message will never be heard. Finally, if your having a huge rally of American Freedom and you allow someone in your group to hold up a black panther or KKK sign then the news is not going to show anything else but those signs and who are holding them up. The absolute best example of this is the Anti-Fascist who call themselves ANTIFA who are not only hypocritical in both their message and actions as they are being fascist while attacking non-fascist with fascism, They themselves are Fascist. Pure idiotic existence no matter how you look at them and their mission.
    III. Always treat a news agency, interview, or questions as always trying to twist your truth, find your arrogance, to either demonize you and your mission or to twist the truth of your mission. We say this not to have you in a defensive mode all the time but

to make sure you are aware of what you say, and how you say it. A good rule of thumb is to be calm, restate the question asked of you, pause and answer the question with only the truth from your "*Know your mission statement always*".

IV. Auditory fluctuations are just as important as optics: Your passion, confidence and sense of purpose comes across in your tone of voice everytime. Thus again the importance of knowing and practicing your mission/message presentation in all the timing windows as in knowing your mission above. Practice over enunciating your words, it will come across better across on video that if your mumbling answers. Push answers from your heart and spirit always, that is the essence of who you are and why your on your mission in the first place. So not knowing the exact questions will prove beneficial to you in making people want to hear what you got to say.

V. Eye Contact: Never look at the camera, but always with the reporter regardless of where they tell you to look. Maintain eye contact with them and do your best to not allow your eyes to wonder left, right or away because these are signs of being dishonest, And again keep your mind on your mission and message always because this will help keep you from being sidetracked into other topics that your not there to discuss, as well as keep you from rolling your eyes at questions that are aimed elsewhere.

VI. Finally, stay calm. The more you practice your message/mission the more calm you will be in an interview situation.

- Press Conferences are a necessity when you begin to work with communications at local, state, and federal levels. They are and can be a great tool to not only state your or your groups position, but for upcoming events, and or issues needing spotlighted. Here are some keys to writing your Press Release;
- List all your "talking points" in your message, then write your release where it takes about 7 min to read through, or

less. Anymore than that you begin to lose attention of the listeners, and 7 min is about the perfect timing when people want to know more or want to ask questions.

- Always expect questions so know what your only going to answer at this press conference ahead of time. Short and concise answers.
- No more that two speakers at your press conference, having multiple speakers usually loses messaging impact to the listener.
- Stats, data, and visual aids are always good at a press conference.
- Always try to check off these parts of your message with writing it; Timing, Significance, Proximity, and Human Interest. All of these areas of your messaging is where most questions will come from.
- Finally it is good to develop a "press kit" for your up and coming press conference. This is a form of a commercial, or preview of your press conference to get the news there. The parts of a press kit are a Summary, Bios of presenters or of whom the message is about, some key facts and data in general, and contact information and of course times and location of the conference.

"Communication is key to the mutual understanding of each of us, and ultimately the life beating heart of unity itself, of a people."

~Yggdrasker

"Now that you have communications down for both yourself, and any size groups in the future. What about your local tribe? When your mission grows in attention from the friendships of those brothers and sisters that you sparked a fire into, that you gave them purpose, now how do you organize? When do you organize? This book you hold in your hands, holds that knowledge, read, it is on your shoulders now to know. Read, be that warrior, that patriot."

STARTING AND OPERATING A
WE THE PEOPLE GROUP

Introduction

The following are ideas and best practices for starting a new group. These are all suggestions that you may or may not use in addition to your own ideas. It is important that your new group reflect your passions, patriotism, and philosophy in winning back our republic. This basic foundation within the overall movement sets itself on our Nation's moto "E Pluribus Unum"

(From the many, One) One Nation, One People, "We The People".

"I wrote this section on how to start a group when I was working with one of the nation's largest movements of the people, the national Tea Party Patriots. I turned it into them and they edited and added this for their own handbook at that time. I rewrote some parts in this version and updated some of it. I give much thanks and admiration to them as I was able to gain so much experience in working with all 50 states and gaining first-hand knowledge on how each group worked in different parts of the country. Tea Party Patriots I salute you for that opportunity you gave me."

Starting and Operating a Group Checklist is a must, there has been a ton of trial and error in this effort throughout many years and the following is our best assessed example of just such a list.

- ❏ Create an organizing committee
- ❏ Group name and purpose
- ❏ Mission statement
- ❏ Establish the organization
- ❏ Develop an image
- ❏ Connect to Tea Party Patriots, and other long time citizens groups with experience
- ❏ Set up communications
- ❏ Get members
- ❏ Make a fundraising plan
- ❏ Identify meeting place and time
- ❏ Promote meetings
- ❏ Prepare a meeting agenda
- ❏ Running the meeting

❑ Retain members

Create an Organizing Committee

- Not impossible to go it alone, but best practice to find help in starting the group.

- Brainstorm and be mindful of steps of which needs to be taken to develop a strong foundation. (follow the check list)

- By doing this your creating an atmosphere of team building, and a responsibility of sharing and communicating from the start.

- This sharing/communications will aid in stopping burn out before it even starts.

- Brainstorm basic structuring and themes of the group itself.

- This way, the opening presentation to the group is one of vision placed firmly with a sense of purpose, rather than just hosting a chaotic free-for-all complaint session.

- Also, without this basic structure in place, you might lose a lot of potential movers and shakers that thrive on mission statements at that first meeting. Remember: first impressions last.

Group Name and Purpose

This is really up to your individual group. Some things to keep in mind:

- You can be named anything you want, so make it identify who you are.

- Identify the real peoples movement, it is a SINGLE movement = We The People.

- We are not a political party, we consist of all parties and no parties.

- Do not make your name discrediting to the movement or have it portray what we are not.

- Please refrain from curse words and bad signage or symbols.

- Understand that we are fighting for our core principle as stated in the introduction, and some key words might be: Liberty, Freedom, Constitution, or We the People.

- Note: Some group names are protected by trademark law, such as Tea Party Patriots. To include those phrases as part of your name, you need permission from the trademark holder.

- Brainstorming about your group's purpose is important to give you some direction. The purpose does not need to be complex or set in stone. You will get more focused as you develop a mission plan, but the purpose will help you get there

- This is your vision

Mission Statement

- You should create a mission statement at the first or second official meeting.

- The mission statement is what defines your group to outsiders researching your group, like prospective future members, the press, and any opposition.

- It also directs the main focus of the mission of the group every time they read it.

- If your group members develop it from scratch, the sense of ownership really comes forth and empowers those participating in it.

- Some key rules of thumb for your mission statement should be:

  - Keep it short; one paragraph at the shortest and two at the most.

  - Define the actual mission.

  - Clear vision for the future.

  - Communicate the values of the group.

  - Will help to guide the behavior of the group.

  - It should be positive.

  - It should be inspiring.

  - Mission statement examples can be found at the end of this document.

Establish an Organization

- A Legal Organization

  - You will need to determine what kind of legal organization you want to be: for profit, not for profit, LLC, corporation, 501(c)(3), 501(c)(4), Political Action Committee (PAC), etc. This will be determined by your activities, be it educational, or political, and your desire for tax exemption or for profit. You will want to consult with an attorney or accountant to determine what will best fit your group.

  - There are also a lot of very successful groups that "operate as a non-profit" organization they decide not to be connected to any governmental agencies for a multiple of reasons. The key here is always remind your membership this is the way it is and any actions by an individual inside or outside of the organization is 100% on their shoulders as far as accountability goes.

o   It is best practice to do one of the above mentioned, however, never just allow one person to take care of financials alone as even if they are the best person in the world there will always be accountability issues needing addressed and It is best practice to have all board members and or leadership controlling all funds.

- Organizational Structure

   o   Your loosely organized organizing committee, will likely be your primary leadership as you get started, but it is important to develop a clear structure early on. This may consist of a governing board with multiple subcommittees, leadership offices that are elected.

   o   Most state laws allow individuals to serve simultaneously in some or all of these roles.

   o   Once you have the leadership structure, and a few meetings under your belt, begin organizing subcommittees. These subcommittees will help spread the workload so the leadership is not doing everything and will provide focus for specific members.

   o   Some subcommittee ideas:

   o   Fundraising · Education · Programs · Events · Outreach · Communications · Public Relations etc.

Develop an Image

- You may not be a big corporation or may not be selling a major product, but a strong image and branding is just as important to a successful liberty group as it is to Coke or Apple. If you want to attract members and volunteers, and have a strong influence within your community and state, you must develop a strong image.

- Leading by example, it is very important to not only know but to actually act upon. For example:

    o Finding out a community need and setting up a table in the name of your group to help and aid in that need. Such as, a member of the community home just burned down so your group leads a drive to help with family. A school team in need of new helmets and your group aides in that endeavor. Its all about "Community relations".

    o Asking city officials to come speak to your group just for information purposes. Not to talk about issues but to speak on who they are and what is their responsibilities are. School Board members, Sheriffs, Police Chiefs, Mayor, City counsel members, City parks and rec, etc.

- Branding

    o Logo

    o Find a good graphic designer.

    o Your logo should be simple and clean. It should express who you are. It should be bold enough to attract your base, but generic enough to attract the general public.

    o Likewise it should not turn off the general public and infuriate your opposition. While this might be fun, it will not further your cause.

- You could register your logo as a trademark.

- Come up with a catchphrase or theme that quickly tells people who you are, unless your name already does this. The catchphrase may be a part of your mission statement.

- Produce some basic materials that you can give to the general public to begin branding your group. For example:

  o · Business Cards · Signage for meetings and other events · Brochure(s) · Signature lines for emails · Letterhead · Bumper

  Stickers · Promotional items such as swag and other giveaway

  items

Connect to other grassroot groups

- Connect to other grassroot groups and their Organization

  o Connect with groups that dedicated to the direct support of grassroots liberty groups throughout the country.

  o Assess the groups and make sure that THE individuals and MEMBERS OF THESE GROUPS ARE THE GRASSROOTS. Grassroots = We The People

  o Start with other local groups, then seek out any within your county, then statewide, before searching for good strong national groups.

- Connect on line, in person, by email, and phone calls. Utilize all forms of communications. Network, network, and oh ya, network.

Communications of Group

- Set Up Communications

- Communication is key to all success. Without communication, the group or mission will fail. At the first meeting, make sure you have either a card or handout that has your contact information as well as that of any other leaders. Those who want to contact you further after your meeting will be able to do so. There are a few best practice communication ideas listed in detail in the communications portion of this handbook. These include:

  - Having sign up sheets and how it is important to keep them private

  - Always Blind-Copy (BCC) in membership blast via email

  - Encourage all group members to build individual lists (word of mouth technique)

  - Phone trees and emergency contact lists

  - Conference calls

  - Websites both TPPs and or your own

  - News letters and blogs

Getting Members and Encouraging Others

- Get Members

  - Your group will not accomplish much if it does not have members. The size of your group is up to you.

Bigger is not always better. Your mission statement and group purpose should help you to determine how big you want to be. If you want to have a strong public presence in your community, you will need a lot of members. If you want to focus on specific policies and quietly lobby for those policies, you may want to be a smaller group.

- o Create an outreach committee early on in your group's creation to begin immediately reaching out to other groups, social media, friends, family, and neighbors to attract members.

- o Always network. Networking, meeting new people, and knowing your group's needs are always key to gaining membership.

Funding

- Funding Meetings
  - o Many groups can fund their basic meeting needs by:
    - Charging a couple of dollars to attend the meeting
    - 50/50 drawings
    - Selling books and other materials at the meetings
    - Selling ad space in emails, meeting programs, etc.
    - Finding businesses or other organizations to sponsor event/s
    - Asking for donations
    - Having silent auctions using donated items
    - Being creative in finding other methods

o   When raising money with any of the ideas listed above, be sure to check local and state laws regarding selling items, raffles, sponsorships, etc. Some states restrict or prohibit these activities.

o   Note: be careful of having dues for your group as that causes a drop off in membership. It is good to have a donation jar etc during each meeting and remind the group to donate if they so wish but leave it at that. You will be surprised by some donations at different times.

Funding Events

- Funding Events

    o   Larger events may require a more aggressive fundraising plan. Specific events such as conferences can often be funded by:

    o   Ticket sales

    o   Product sales

    o   Businesses or sponsorships from other organizations

    o   Elected representatives will often sponsor events, especially during an election year. Be sure to check state and federal laws, particularly if yours is a nonprofit group that must avoid any appearance of endorsing a candidate.

Other Areas To Consider

- Topics initially needing discussed:

    o   Meeting place and time

- Promoting meetings
- Preparing a meeting agenda
- Running a meeting
- And Retaining members which some listed are:
    - Provide leadership opportunities
    - Delegate
    - Be an active group
    - Keep your members growing
    - Seek out talents and strengths and use them
    - Seek input Pickle jar technique.

"There are many important steps and best practices for starting and maintaining a tribe or clan, but the most important things to remember are to be creative, think outside the box, and make it your own. Each We The People group is unique and has their own strengths and weaknesses. That is the beauty of the liberty movement; it consists of many Americans from all walks of life coming together to promote the America Dream."

~Yggdrasker

"As a citizen of the United States you must know that it is We The People who set up our government, that the government is subservient to We The People, that the POWER of our government 100% comes from We The People, as it is We The People, who are the highest authority within our government. This is called Popular Sovereignty."

KEY UNDERSTANDINGS

"WE THE PEOPLE"

MUST KNOW

Santa Maria Vs Mayflower

Now clear your mind and allow what your about to read sink in.

Christopher Columbus took 91 people aboard three ships; the Nina, the Pinta, and the Santa Maria from Polos de la Frontera on August 3rd, 1492. They landed in the Bahamas archipelago, "Central America" on <u>October 12th, 1492.</u>

The Puritans and the Pilgrims took 130 people aboard the Mayflower alone and cramped, on September 16th, 1620. They landed and set anchor near the tip of Cape Cod, "North America" on <u>November 21st, 1620</u>.

Time and area differences between these two voyages are eye opening to the truth of the development of the United States and the mentality between the two.

"October 12th 1492" to "November 21st, 1620" = 128 years.

128 years is two lifetimes, two generations! It is a shame that most Americans cannot even site the names of those famous ships and who sailed them, but worse, some believe the Mayflower was just a part of Columbus's fleet. This ignorance leads to the belief that all Europeans (white man) came to steal land, wealth, and power. To concur and make the world their kingdom.

Nothing could be further from the truth.

So from the Kings and Queens of Spain, France, Portugal, and their mentality of conquering the world through their monarchies, and their practice of the inquisition mindset grew throughout Central and South America. England did not even reach the New World until 1607 and started Jamestown in Virginia as their first colony way north of the others. Although still with the same mentalities as the other Monarchies, yet still 13 years prior to the Mayflower's arrival.

So in all out accuracy, none of the above can begin the story of the "Beginning" of the United States of America", nor should they be, and the following is why.

You see, the entire reason of the Puritans and Pilgrims voyage was actually more of an escape. An escape of religious persecution from the European Monarchies. They literally sought a start in a new land far away from any King or the Vatican to be able to worship freely as they preached and prayed in fear of their lives. So yes they set sail to go as far away as they could to the well-established colony of Virginia.

Then something happened, they could not reach Virginia as a

storm blew them off course further to the north and anchored near the Cape Cod area. But they simply did not just get off the ship onto shore. They knew they had to be governed somehow. So they came up with a contract, a mini constitution, a compact that all agreed to before leaving the ship. **The Mayflower Compact.** Which clearly states they set foot only for the advancement of the Christian faith, and advancement of freedom away from the tyrannical forced version they fled from. You see this compact was a first of its kind. An experiment if you will, an exercise in consensual government among themselves. A bond of understanding to work with each other and depend not on a king or queen or the Vatican for survival, but to work for and lean on each other to make it.

Many experiments of governing were tried and attempted after this monumental beginning. It wasn't until September 17th, 1787 that the United States Constitution was signed. That is two more lifetimes, two more generations from the landing of the Mayflower. 167 years later.

The importance of this knowledge is to know that the United States of America was not made to concur as a part of a tyrannical governance system, but quite the opposite, to be a foundation of a free united society. Many historical events and history proves this to be so, such as the colony of Providence Rhode Island established n 1636 as a haven for religious dissenters. Here white, black, Indian, and Asians lived as equals, brothers and sisters. So many more examples is in our beginnings.

"One thing we have found throughout the history of mankind is that corruption is a twisted and manipulated purposeful act by those in charge. And quite often they do so my small acts of deceit going unnoticed until they build on top of the stage they set beneath your own feet. This small manipulation of definitions is just the most common."

Democracy VS Republic

The 1828 Websters Dictionary defines Popular Sovereignty as: *"a doctrine in political theory that government is created by and subject to the will of the people"*

So let us look at both a Democracy and a Republic and see first, that these are two very distinct different forms of government and should not be used interchangeably, and second, which form actually takes away the sovereignty of the people.

Democracy

The 1828 Webster's Dictionary defines democracy as: *"Government by the people; a form of government, in which the supreme power is lodged in the hands of the people collectively, or in which the people exercise the powers of legislation. Such was the government of Athens."* Sounds as if popular sovereignty fits here just fine. Lets continue shall we.

A democracy form of government is where there are ruling positions that are elected by a majority of the citizenship. Then those elected in office become in charge of the people and develop legislation/laws to govern said people. In other words a rule of a majority faction of the people. A part of the citizenship that compartmentalizes themselves and that just so happens to outnumber the other citizens. You see it is a tribal mindset or party mindset which creates divisions and outright competition for the power to rule. This mindset steals away the sovereignty of We The People.

This was most simply put by Benjamín Franklin when he said: *"Democracy is **two wolves and a lamb** voting on what to have for lunch. Liberty is a well-armed *lamb* contesting the vote."* This is NOT what America is, nor should be, as this clearly takes away from the sovereignty of the people.

Republic

The 1828 Webster's Dictionary defines a Republic as: *"A commonwealth; a state in which the exercise of the sovereign power is lodged in representatives elected by the people. In modern usage, it differs from a democracy or democratic state, in which the people exercise the powers of sovereignty in person. Yet the democracies of Greece are often called republics."* Now this most definitely fits both the popular in people being accurately represented as a whole and the sovereignty of the citizens where by the citizens ensures their representatives speaks accurately for them.

Where a democracy champions the will of the mob rule, a Republic champions the rights of each individual citizen. We The People cannot forget this truth, nor wrap our minds around its actions. You see the difference is that in a Republic those we vote into office are truly the voice of their constituency. Meaning We The People must stay engaged in communications with the elected official so there is no question of who he/she speaks for. If We The People do this the elected always reminded of their place and will do their duty in service. A great example of this was during the signing of the Declaration of Independence, of the 13 colonies represented the vote to approve it were 12 yeas and 1 abstained. Why wasn't it 13 unanimous? Because Mr. Lewis Morris who was present for New York Colony never did receive word back from his constituency on time for the vote. Now if the time had the mindset of a democracy Morris would of gladly took it upon himself to make the decision and vote yea. Even though the American constitution was not yet written, this example was exactly one We The People can use to exercise the action within a Republic.

James Madison explained this concept by saying: *"A republic, by which I mean a government in which the scheme of representation takes place, opens a different prospect, and promises the cure for which we are seeking."*

And this one By Thomas Jefferson with he said: *"A democracy is nothing more than mob rule, where fifty-one percent of the people may take away the rights of the other forty-nine."*

This is exactly the mentality of our nation's politics in the early 2000's, and this is exactly why We The People need to defend the Constitution.

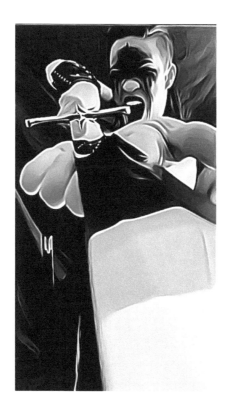

"Diversity is the driving force that leads to divisions in America. For whatever reason, educators, through society, stole the definition from one word, then used it to define diversity, then demanded and even force the people to be obedient to it, which has only divided We The People further than ever. One cannot use the definition of one word and force it upon another word meaning the opposite, without a damaging outcome. This is truth, and this is exactly what has been done here. What was the word they stole the definition from? University."

Diversity Vs University

Diversity

You see the meaning of diversity comes from the specific root of "Diverse" in Latin, it is a verb that means "to turn aside". This same root gave us our English verb "to divert", or "divorce," you know, where people can "turn away" a spouse. In Latin, the participle form of diversity is "diversus" which came to mean "separate," and finally filtered through old French, became "diverse" meaning "separate" or "different". Sense the 15th and 16th centuries it's been used to mean the quality of "deviating from accepted behavior," i.e., being wrong or evil.

So take the understanding of all you just learned; diverse, to turn aside, to divert, divorce, turn away, diversus, separate, different, deviating from accepted behavior. All of these create a direct understanding that to push and force "Diversity" is to turn away, separate, segregate, hyphenate, and compartmentalize the American people. White America, Black America, Rich America, Poor America, Male America, Female America, Straight America, Gay America, Religious America, Pagan America, To force Diversity is to Divide We The People, and it has been so now for decades.

Look and understand the word they are stealing the definition from is "University".

University

If you look into the root of "university" you see "universe", meaning the sum of everything, the cosmos, "everything" does not matter the differences within all, it is "all in one". That Latin word "universe" combined "vertere" which means "to turn" with "uni" which means "one". So universe means "to turn into one". The word "university" in our modern academia sense, dates to the 14th century, and originally was used to define the gathering of various scholarly societies, guilds, student bodies and the like with one organization of learning, Universities. So in other words they define the action of taking multiple different types of one thing, in this case areas of study, and putting them together in one place of study, is called a University.

So now take the understanding of all you just learned from University; universe, everything, all in one, vertere, uni, one, to turn into, university. All of these create a total different understanding than diversity, where here, when you study and educate yourself with "University" you in fact accept all together, to marry, turn all things different into one, equal to all, and identified as a single unit or component.

"Sounds kind of familiar, does it not?"

Is that not our Nation's moto? E Pluribus Unum (from the many, one). We are "One Nation Under God", a "Melting Pot", "One People", "One Human Race", "One America", "One Law", and yes "We The People", all representing a UNITED citizenship for One Nation. Respecting all backgrounds, and heritage and becoming one in university, one in love and respect, Not diversity where we identify a separate America, a compartmentalized America.

Why would anyone want to continue to <u>divide</u> our Nation by pushing <u>different</u> Americas' by pushing <u>Diversity</u>? We need to stop and regroup and begin to stoke the fires of freedom, liberty and one America, by doing that which <u>unites</u> the people, by pushing <u>University</u>!

"If there is anything my people know is that from the beginning of humankind there is no people that are innocent of gaining lands of other people and nations. That all peoples even those getting their lands taken from themselves are not innocent of this action. That is not said as a justification, only an acknowledgment of the nature of man. Your land here in America is no different, and as we can write a whole story just on this we will save that for another day. However, the aforementioned is necessary to understand when we talk of this nation as it exists today. The genius of this newly created Constitution of the United States has come by way of studying the best of all prior tried governments by people and nations from around the world and history. To include some very native American influence. Read, understand, that the law of the land is very much unbiased in its development for peace, equality, and unity."

Iroquois and the Constitution

The natives at the time of discovery of America were many tribes also with many different beliefs, foundations, and leadership amongst themselves. Many tribes befriended and helped the Europeans from the very beginning and in many areas such as how to plant different types of vegetables, and other foods, and medicines from local plants as well as fishing techniques that the strangers have never seen before. Just as many Europeans returned the favor by showing latest in technology of their time, and iron works etc. Many examples from the long time inhabitants of this land were very influential to the making of America. One such example comes from the Iroquois Confederacy which was made up of the Cayuga, Mohawk, Onondaga, Oneida, Seneca, and the Tuscarora Nations. The Iroquois Confederation called themselves "People Building a Long House." Or Haudenosaunee.

Benjamin Franklin who attended the Confederacy treaty councils wrote of it in 1736 in his printing business. Franklin very much intrigued by the unity government of the Iroquois, brought the concept in strict conviction with him to the Constitutional Convention some 40 years later.

You see each of these separate tribes within the Iroquois Confederacy all were sovereign to themselves governed by themselves but all 6 of these nations came together as one in unity in national defense and in natural disasters. The overall governing constitution of the Iroquois nation that influenced the American Constitution are as follows; Restricts members from holding more than one office in the Confederacy. Outlines processes to remove leaders within the Confederacy. Designates two branches of legislature with procedures of passing laws. Describes who has the power to declare war. Creates a balance of power between the Confederacy and individual tribes.

All of these areas can very easily be found in the United States Constitution as well. In 1744, Chief Canassatego of the Onondaga tribe gave a speech while pleading the 13 colonies to unite under a similar constitution as of the Iroquois Confederation. At that treaty conference sat no other but Benjamin Franklin who like the genius he was, wrote the Chief's speech on paper for future value. Here are the words of Chief Canassatego;

"We heartily recommend Union and a good Agreement between you our Brethren...Never disagree, but preserve a strict Friendship for one

another, and thereby you, as well as we, will become the stronger. Our wise Forefathers established Union and Amity between the Five Nations; this has made us formidable; this has given us great Weight and Authority with our neighboring Nations. We are a powerful Confederacy; and, by your observing the same Methods our wise Forefathers have taken, you will acquire fresh Strength and Power; therefore whatever befalls you, never fall out one with another."

Chief Canassatego used a visual teaching method the elders used to school their own children at this meeting with our founders took place. He held up one arrow, and told those looking on that this is but one tribe, if you put pressure upon it to destroy it, it will only be able to withstand so much before it is shattered and defeated. He then picked up a handful of arrows, say 13, and bound them together with a common law and commitment to one another. He then picked out the strongest man in the meeting and asked him to try and break the united bundle of arrows. He could not. This is the secret to the defense and security of peace. You all now know, its called university.

In 1988 the Senate of the United States Congress passed a resolution respecting the influence of the Iroquois Confederacy to your Constitution when it states;

"The confederation of the original 13 colonies into one republic was influenced by the political system developed by the Iroquois Confederacy, as were many of the democratic principles which were incorporated into the constitution itself."

There was many pieces that were not used from the Iroquois Confederacy but the overall concept and mildly tweaked details, there is no debate on the truth behind a great inspiration from the native peoples into our weaving the fabric of our beloved country.

Now do not allow anyone to preach how the Constitution of the United States is racist. It is weaved with the spirit of unity of all peoples to become one as a nation.

Electoral College

First of all the Electoral College is not a place of study, it is a process. Let me explain, You see our founding fathers established the concept and made sure it was a part of the Constitution of the United States. They had to come up with this concept to answer the dilemma of the popular votes in larger dense populations would eventually decide who our president was each and every time. Basically not giving colonies (states) with smaller populations a voice when elections are held.

So they came up with the Electoral College to compromise and make sure that every state had a voice and definite representation in choosing our president.

The Electoral College process consists of 538 electors. Of the 538 electors a candidate must gain 270 or better to gain the majority to be elected. Each state has the same number of electors as it has Congressional House Representatives and Senators. 1 for each House Reps, and 1 for each of the two Senators.

Finally, each candidate or candidate's party has their own "slate" or set of electors. Those electors become the official electors after their candidate wins the popular vote of their state. Then the 270 or better electors actually are the winning candidate's slate of electors.

This process and practice keeps all 50 states and the district of Columbia on an equal playing field with a fair representation of voices. Without this process, there would be no reason for most states to participate in the election at all, due to the popular or mob majority vote would be dominated by the very liberal blue states of NY and CA.

Prepping and Survival

What does Prepping mean? Why is it important and When should I start?

Prepping is just being prepared. Its that simple. It is like your auto, or life insurance. Its there if something goes terribly wrong, hopefully you will never have to use it, BUT if it does it is there if you need it. Unfortunately, a lot of people in today's society have never experienced a need to be prepared and tend to keep kicking the can down the road or worse yet, think its nuts to go to such lengths because everything is just fine. These mindsets lead people to underestimate the *possibility of disaster*, and the harmful effects of a disaster *as it is happening*. Prepping is the act of preparing for a dangerous and harmful event before it happens. Disaster comes in different forms, environmental, financial, societal and political. Such as Hurricanes, Ice Storms, the loss of your job or source of major income, and the most unpredictable a pandemic or political and civil unrest.

You may have heard of TEOTWAWKI an acronym for "The End Of The World As We Know It". We live in an unprecedented time that TEOTWAWKI could be around the corner. Like the generations before us that lived through the cold war with Russia, we must be prepared to protect and provide for our families if conventional ways of accessing resources are unavailable. I urge my fellow Americans to not leave the responsibility of your family's survival to anyone else other than yourself.

If you have not been following multiple news sources that cover national and international reporting, you may not be aware of how important it is, *to not wait one more day to start prepping.* If what you learn on the news does not concern you enough to consider prepping, I want you to imagine a world event that shut everything down. Suppose the power grid goes down for instance. No power grid = no electricity= no communication = no mobile phone, = no computer, = no information about what is happening, and no way to get help. Now image days go by and people have begun to panic because they are running out of food and water. Some people are out of life saving medications like insulin, heart and blood pressure medications, and people are starting to die. In less than 30 days the 7.2% of American adults that require anti-depressant medication are out of theirs and their behavior is no longer regulated, alcohol, cigarettes and street drugs becomes scarce. Chaos has officially set in people are desperate and you are now one of them, because you were not prepared. What are you going to be forced to do to survive? Will you even be physically able to do anything or just become a victim? Who is going to take care of your family?

Before we go there lets see a truth that we are experiencing right now, at the time this handbook is being created, shall we?

We are seeing actions being forced upon us as if there actually is a pandemic, even though the effects of an actual pandemic is not happening and the level of leverage against society is nowhere near what it could be, But that is not stopping the government to force pandemic controls on the people creating a domino effect overall a scenario that if not stopped will cause a need to be well prepared for what will come.

What we know comes naturally and instinctively in a real pandemic situation is that those forced actions leads to large scale quarantines and business shutdowns, which leads to the destruction of our economy. Which triggers economic ruin and the increase in crimes and chaos that could lead to martial law. As that country continues on in its unstableness we soon see civil unrest that leads to tribal and civil war style chaos which could trigger enemy nations to take their steps in attacking the U.S.A. with EMP (electromagnetic pulse) attacks as well as infiltration to our already weak governmental administration. Now you may not see all this happening, but as we can see at the moment, it is far more likely than not at this point.

So what do we do to prepare? How do we make a first move? This handbook will give an understanding and a guidance on setting those goals. We will give a basic foundation that you need to adhere to, and begin research to begin your prepping. Continuethemission.net has a whole page dedicated to that endeavor. As we find more bloggers to contribute it will be a great place to start. As there are others out there as well.

The first rule of thumb you need to understand is your current self-assessment, your current environment, and location. These all create an either strong or weak foundation for We The People nationwide. It is imperative that you embrace this fact and begin at the first level of development and move up as you go. So let us begin.

1. *Yourself*
Look inside of yourself first and foremost. Why? Because you, you are a link within a unity of One People, and if you are negative, weak, spoiled, or rotten then you put the unity of your people as a whole in jeopardy. No one is perfect, and everyone has room to improve themselves from within, find your weakness and improve, strengthen that which bogs you down. Then as you find your strengths and perfect them and share your knowledge and wisdom, you do so with a heart of a nation, our country. My new friends, find your Faith, better your Health, and repair your Character. This, this is your first step in

preparation and restoring our "E Pluribus Unum."

2. *Family, Home, and Property*

Once you have yourself in order, use your Character to lead
by example. Now your focus is improving, strengthen and
prepping your family, your home and your property. Why?
Because just as important as it was to repair yourself for
the unity of your people, your family, home, and property
also must be restored to keep yourself and family safe. A
very important and forgotten truth is that the ownership of
property gives We The People power to resist tyranny of a
greater power. Today's liberals and extreme leftists try to
teach that our founders were greedy and selfish only when
land ownership comes to focus. But our founders knew that
property ownership can be used as a tactical leverage in gaining
said power. So they designed a self governed Republic can
do just that, own property with a leverage of power over the
government from taking power away from the people. We The
People must prep their homes and property to the maximum
ability they are able to. In general, make sure you have enough
prepped items such as food, water, medicines, and weapons to
maintain you and your family for at least 3 to 4 months, at all
times. Granted the size of your home determines how much
prep you can store, but the truth remains, you must prep as
if to stay self sustained in your home for as long a period you
able to prep for. This prep is for any circumstances that may
occur. Natural disasters, home quarantines, chaos in the streets,
military martial law imposed, or simply put, an attack from
those seeking to take away your personal freedoms. Today
as extreme leftist globalist college professors try to debunk or
rewrite a quote from a WWII Japanese general who said, " *You
cannot invade the mainland United States. There would be a rifle
behind every blade of grass"* as those leftist globalist try to stop
any inspiration for our right to own guns, the truth within that
quote is in fact a strategic detail. If We The People continue
to prep our homes and property to the utmost to sustain their
families, they are in essence creating every home (blade of
grass) as a stronghold, a bunker in itself if you will. But most
importantly, a safe place you and your family can be at peace.

Let me be very clear here, this level of prepping is for you, your family, and your power, not any other focus. The level of possible combatives can come from multiple elements outside your property, and anyone who says this is a prep to create an army outside our government, or any other stupid comment like that, is only trying to demonize you for doing the right thing in prepping for your security and safety. Again the emphasis is on you making your family and property safe and developing a defense mechanism to protect your freedoms and liberty.

Some basic rules to use while prepping is the following:

The rule of Three

Survival rate: 3 minutes without air, 3 hours exposed in harsh environment, 3

days without drinkable water and 3 weeks without food.

The rule of three is the golden rule for prepping in every aspect. An example

is, if you only have one way to make a fire, say a lighter and it run out, you

have no way to make fire. If you have a lighter and waterproof match, you

now have one way to make fire in case one fails. If you have a lighter,

waterproof matches, and flint and steel wool, you now have two ways to

make fire in case one way fails. You should always do your best to have three

ways to provide for yourself in every aspect of your prep.

Basic Prepping Priorities

Here is a basic list of what you should be prepared for.

1. *Drinkable Water- Purification and Storage*
2. *Ability to make fire*
3. *Safe shelter*
4. *Food- Storage and the ability to grow or hunt for it.*
5. *Medical*
6. *Safety-Ability to protect yourself and your prep*
7. *Communications*
8. *A trusted Network of peers*

3. *Networking with neighbors, friends, and family.*

This is all found in the "*A guide to communications and networking*" and the "*Starting and Operating a We The People group*". This phase should be accomplished as soon as #1 and #2 are complete. You have got to understand that these are foundational building methods and best practices. Don't jump to #3 before building the other two first. With that said, it brings us to a fourth and very important phase of making We The People stronger, in unity, and stronger in as E Pluribus Unum.

4. *The Constitutional Militia Solution is the 4th phase of prepping after 1-3 are accomplished.*

Below.

THE CONSTITUTIONAL MILITIA SOLUTION

"The key to this very fundamental aspect of your rights and freedoms given to you by God himself is very well written and straight forward in your 2ⁿᵈ Amendment in the Constitution of the United States. So lets begin there first so you truly understand its meaning before going into what I believe how it was supposed to unfold."

The Second Amendment

"A well regulated militia, being necessary to the security of a free state, the right of the people to keep and bear arms, shall not be infringed."

"A well regulated militia," Ended with a comma, a coma is used to pause between a thought where a period ends the thought. So, that is the first thing we must realize within this one sentence Amendment.

"A well regulated militia", Regulated by who? The State? Nope.

The Federal Government? Wrong again. The militia is to be well regulated by those who are forming the militia, We The People.

"being necessary to the security of a free state," again ending in a comma, a pause to point out it is a necessity, what is a necessity? A well regulated militia, by the people, is necessary to what? A secure themselves, their family, and property which is a free state.

"the right of the people to keep and bear arms," again just a pause to make the point that it is the right of who? The Government people? Nope. The State government people? Nope. "The People" all the people, all American citizens have the right to bear arms to form a well regulated militia protect themselves, their families, and property to secure all of their state so all can be free.

"shall not be infringed." Now finally a period, ending this amendment with the strong statement "shall no be infringed." Infringed? To actively break these terms, or law. What terms? 1. The action of a Well regulated militia 2. Necessity of people forming a well regulated militia to keep it free. 3. The right of the people to own the arms to form a well regulated militia. And 4. No laws or terms to change any of the aforesaid. None. It is a simple as that. The constitution of the United States of America is the ONLY license one needs to own a carry arms. And until an amendment is brought forth on this matter all other laws and regulations are unconstitutional. Period.

So what would be a natural and more accurate interpretation or explanation of who and how and when a militia should be formed? From the mindset of our founders and the context of all justifications put forth what might be a best practice here?

So we first discussed a self-assessment and self-preparedness in starting to build a strong foundation. Starting here is a must, yes a duty to arm yourself with what you feel comfortable in doing so with. It is essential in finding your strengths and talents in all aspects of your life, and self-defense is one of them. Your choice of arms is totally up to you. It is not mandated, however, your self-assessment should bring you to an understanding of what level of self-defense your capable of. This is okay, whatever that level turns out to be, that is why it is We The People, that comes in play later.

Next as we spoke of is preparing your family, home, and property, so here arms for members of your family, training, and proper storage of your arms, ammo, as well as your food, water, and medicines. Role play scenarios around your property and home with your family, discuss dos and don'ts, best practices in defense of your home. How would you break into your home and then plan on how you would defend against that. All of this is a good thing, and best practice to help you prepare for the worse God forbid of course.

After these are done is when the reaching out to your family, friends and neighbors to hopefully bring them all on board with a communication understanding, and neighborhood watch scenario if you will, and everyone in your area preparing on their own for their piece of freedom, or properties and homes. All tie together in unity. When this is being done, it would be a great time to starting and operating your own We The People Group. Follow those best practices set forth for you and within that group, you will begin a group assessment and find from your people, your members, those that will be in local government, those that will focus on state government and national government. You will also find those within your group to coordinate and form rallies at all levels, you will find those to coordinate and form financial fund raising efforts to raise money for your groups service to your community and area. You will find those who will plan, form and coordinate events of all kinds that will benefit your community and area. And you will find those within your group to coordinate, form a well-regulated militia from your members not as a scary army, but to help all get armed, trained, and well-disciplined through love, care and training for a bad situation. Within this group all know who are chosen to lead in whatever area, and the understanding of self-defense, and defense of our freedoms will come together as We The People, all people, from your area. These areas should be on your monthly meetings agenda items to update and discuss. Each has it area of importance and the group never identifies itself as anything but a We The People group. Not a militia, not a political party, but a group of We The People in an area wanting to make a difference and lead by example of how a unified people, a unified citizenship should look like and operate.

So after all this gets underway, the steps taken by the militia members of your group, has the duty to come up with their protocols, chain of command, self-disciplines, uniforms, trainings etc. This is a better understanding of what our forefathers envisioned. Local militias formed from We The People to defend your land from tyranny.

A good checklist to use when deciding what to train for within your militia is the following:

1. *Self-defense, boxing, mma, martial arts, handguns, knives, less lethal munitions like mace, pepper spray etc.*
2. *Home defense, alarm systems, shotguns, handguns, less lethal munitions like beanbag projectiles, kinetic ammunition, pepper balls, boarding up windows, escape routes, communications, fortifications, and safe rooms.*
3. *Property defense, alarm systems, rifles, surveillance, and communication networks.*
4. *Militia level patrols of area, surveillance of community sector (neighborhood watch) authority communications, community value training, public relations. Uniforms, local laws training and networking, gun safety courses and instructor courses to provide service for the community.*

Always be safe, and always stay within the law, and always know and defend the rights of We The People according to the Constitution of the United States.

FOUNDATIONAL INFORMATION NEEDED

"Civics have long been forgotten by your educational system here in America. So much so, that one would even say to your detriment. It is extremely important to reeducate yourselves the details within our Republic to keep it moving. To write all we would need to cover here would need to be an entire book by itself, just to cover said civics and the actions it takes to be effective. I will take that challenge and commit to doing a follow up, a part II if you will to this handbook focused directly on civics. But for now, I will leave a simple 10 question test here, to show you to your own self-assessment how rare it is for any US Citizen today, to actually pass a US Citizenship Test. There are 100 questions that could be asked but from a random 10 questions of the 100 is all that is asked to pass a US Citizenship test. You must get 6 out of 10 correct. This will be a gage for you to see how far behind you are in these basic civic test questions below, that we all should of learned before our graduation of high school, if not earlier. So answer these 10 basic questions and be honest with yourself to do a quick self-assessment. Good luck."

1. *How many amendments does the US Constitution have?*
2. *What is the rule of law?*
3. *Name one of the U.S. Senators of your State.*
4. *Why do some states have more representatives than others?*
5. *What are 2 cabinet level positions?*
6. *The Federalist Papers are supported the passage of the U.S. Constitution. Name one of its authors.*
7. *What did Susan B. Anthony do?*
8. *Who was President during WWI?*
9. *Name one of the two longest rivers in the United States.*
10. *Why does the Flag have 13 stripes?*

Now, be honest with yourself before reading the answers below and honestly score your results.

1. *Twenty-Seven*
2. *Everyone must follow the law. Leaders must obey the law. Government must obey the law. No one is above the law.*
3. *Answers vary so research and see if you got it right.*
4. *The number of state representatives is based on a state's population.*
5. *Again vary depending on who is President at the time this question is being asked. Research your President's administration cabinets to see if you are correct.*
6. *James Madison, Alexander Hamilton, John Jay,*
7. *Fought for women's rights, fought for civil rights.*
8. *Woodrow Wilson*
9. *Mississippi river or the Missouri river.*
10. *The stripes represent the first 13 colonies in our nation.*

"You see it seems to me that the #1 reason of why our Republic is in the shambles it is today, and is the most underlying fabric of decay within our nation, which so often goes undetected, is **slothfulness**. *This diseased mindset keeps the individual citizen from performing their personal duty as a member of We The People. That duty is to be engaged in their local, state, and federal levels of government. There are multiple ways one can do this, and by putting them off, or outright ignoring your duty because it's not exciting or you don't want to get political, then you are allowing the corruption and tyranny to develop within the government and in essence deserve what transforms around you. So let's not do that and look at a small simple list that you can focus on at a minimum and make a huge impact as an authority of our governmental system."*

1. *Yes make sure you vote at all levels, for all offices, where voting is necessary. Vote for your school boards, city councils, state legislatures, and national legislatures. All of which, every single one of them are your servants, your representatives, not the other way around. To do this get to know who is running, what they stand for etc. Below is a* **Candidate assessment score card** *that Gregg Cummings developed to aid in the duty of the American citizens to make sure they vote into service those that truly represent the people. The three Top columns are always constant in your assessments.* <u>Character, Core Values, and Issues</u>. *The way it works is each candidate you assess, you do so by scoring 1-5, 1 being worst and 5 being best, in each area line item under each column. Then you total up the score under each and the candidate with the highest score at the end is and should be your first choice. Then as the*

election continues on, if your #1 candidate drops out for whatever reason, then you do not go home as well, but instead you then start supporting your #2 highest scored candidate, and so on. Then in the end, if all citizens do this, truly the best candidate for the people will rise to the top representing the people with honor.

Assessor Name: Assessor eMail:

We The People Candidate Assessment Report Card

CANDIDATE:

Character	Score 1-5	Core Values	Score 1-5	Issues	Score 1-5	
Honesty/Integrity		Personal Freedom/ Constitutionally Limited Government		Border Security		
Grassroots/of the People		Economic Freedom/ Free Markets		Repeal Obama Care		
Virtue/Principled		Debt Free Future/ Fiscal Responsibility		Eliminate the IRS		
Dependability		Constitutionalist		Defend 2nd Amendment		
Courage		Religious Freedom		Stop Common Core		
Decisive/ Solution Oriented		American Exceptionalism		National Defense/Israel		
Communication		United State Sovereignty		Pro Life		NOTES
Total		Total		Total		

2. *Always learn more about your nation's history and civics, knowledge is truly power. And knowing the three sacred documents of your country (Declaration of Independence, Constitution, and Bill of Rights), is an outstanding place to start moving forward. Knowing these you will be able to hold accountable, always, your elected officials.*

3. *Always speak out at every venue in defense of those same 3 sacred documents. You, we, simply cannot allow any, not even the smallest deviation away from the original intent of our Republic. Not one bill past, not one speech given that is in opposition of our Constitution. Stand up, speak out, write out, blog out, vlog out, meme out, email out, phone call out, office visit out, have a backbone, use your fear of speaking up, and use that energy to motivate yourself. The more you speak up, the easier it gets. Study the communications portion of this handbook and put it into action.*

*Now go and find a good site like www.wallbuilders.
com and
https://www.educatorsathome.com/civics-101/ and
learn as
much civics as you can, then share your knowledge
with others.*

BLACK ROBED REGIMENT

"If you all are reading this book, this handbook of the modern day American Citizen, then you must be as devoted, and passionate about patriotism as I. Is it enough that we only complain about our predicament as a society today? What kind of citizens are we today? Can we act on all the beliefs we hold dear and speak about on a daily basis now? Do you really believe? Do you need some other influence or drive? What needs to happen for you to stand up and proclaim like Patrick Henry did when he said "...as for me, give me liberty or give me death." Is that kind of bravery, commitment to values

alive anymore? Well this book would not be complete without speaking of and telling the story of the black robed regiment. Lets do that."

The British coined this term back in 1775 when they heard and realized pastors and ministers from across the new world are leading a lot of the revolutionary soldiers in battle. They meant it as a derogatory comment however, the title stuck, and those leaders wore it with pride and distinction as it not only showed their commitment to a new free nation but also showed their reliance to the creator of all things. So the black robed regiment was born. But why?

You see, prior to the Declaration of Independence, prior to there being a Revolutionary Army, There were two main areas of which common citizens met, and congregated to communicate of the current events and happenings around their new homelands. Those were the local pubs, and the local churches. Here is how plans were made, coordination were handled, and was indeed the communication hubs of the people.

From these very pulpits of the churches the people would hear what happens to nations that forget God, or how important it was for Godly men to be in charge vs the evil corrupt men of which they fled from in Europe. Look, churches and pubs were the epicenter of issues effecting all the population in those days. And they stood up, encouraged, and freedom and liberty where there was nothing else. The difference between the two is that pubs were groups and in the Churches is was coming hard and strong from the pulpits. These leaders, the pastors and ministers, lead the way, built in all citizens a strong foundation of which courage would thrive. If tyranny

111

was not resisted it would grow like the most aggressive cancer one could imagine. These leaders knew this.

This is were Patrick Henry gave his famous "Give me liberty, or give me death." From the pulpit. Another great quote from one of these Black Robed Reverends that inspired and help justify standing up was Rev. James Caldwell who said *"There are times were it is as righteous to fight, as it is to pray."* and he was very much spot on. Not only was he spot on, every single point made in the Declaration of Independence, although written by Thomas Jefferson, was preached from the pulpits throughout the colonies for years by these courageous, committed, and honorable Pastors, Ministers, and Reverends alike. But now, today, our churches have grown silent for the most part. Seeking refuge to maintain their unconstitutional laws of 501 c3 nonprofit status from our corrupt government. Projecting cowardly reasons to stay quiet and not rock the boat by getting involved in politics. This is wrong. We need those spiritual leaders in our land today to follow the Black Robed Regiment mindset of days gone past. Reestablish E Pluribus Unum, and retake the peoples rightful spot in our Republic, and resist the amount of regulations, unconstitutional laws, and outright tyranny of our current governmental leaders.

Pray yes, Fast yes, Stand Up yes, Speak Out yes, and remember the words from our Declaration of Independence which stands just as true today as it did when they were first written.

"...and for the support of this declaration, with a firm reliance on the protection of Divine Providence, we mutually pledge to

each other our lives, our fortunes, and our sacred honor"

Now go and have a serious sitdown conversation with your pastors, have him look up the current movement of the Black Robed Regiment, and get them to see the honor to God in standing up from the pulpits to save our nation.

I've always had a vision to help veterans and service members. Their courage and selflessness to provide Americans the right of freedom, should be met with equal selflessness when they return home.

I really didn't know how I was going to make my vision a reality.. I only knew that I wanted to. I took my first breath, in Fort Hood, Texas. As a Military brat, America, means more to me than most could ever fathom. My father served in the Army and his father was a pilot in the Army. I was also married into the Marine Corps back in the day. My love for this country the beautiful United States of America as well as for those that serve is relentless.

When I was first introduced to continue the mission, I was very excited! Gregg C. Cummings had created an entire website devoted to helping service members and veterans. The amount of information that he provided and the ways that he helps others, no one could compare.

Gregg took me under his wing, I've learned a lot from him in the time that I've known him. One things for sure, he has a bigger heart than I've ever seen, and passion that surpasses mine for his country and people. And that is a lot to say about someone, being how much I love this country and the people.

Anytime I have needed anything, Gregg has always manage to be there. Whether I had a Vet that was in trouble and needed help talking him off the ledge, or if I was in trouble and just needed help dealing with my own personal life. I am proud and honored to be a part of the RWBNC, As well part of a huge family of patriots that want nothing more than justice, unity and freedom.

Continue the mission is and does exactly as it states.

"Charlie Mike" (Continue the Mission)

SpokesWarrior

Tracy Sirls

The 1776 Report

The President's Advisory 1776 Commission

January 2021

TABLE OF CONTENTS

I. INTRODUCTION 1

II. THE MEANING OF THE DECLARATION...........................2

III. A CONSTITUTION OF PRINCIPLES 6

IV. CHALLENGES TO AMERICA'S PRINCIPLES...................10
SLAVERY...10
PROGRESSIVISM...12
FASCISM...13
COMMUNISM...14
RACISM AND IDENTITY POLITICS...15

V. THE TASK OF NATIONAL RENEWAL 16
THE ROLE OF THE FAMILY..17
TEACHING AMERICA...17
A SCHOLARSHIP OF FREEDOM...18
THE AMERICAN MIND...18
REVERENCE FOR THE LAWS..19

VI. CONCLUSION..20

APPENDIX I: THE DECLARATION OF INDEPENDENCE.............................21

APPENDIX II: FAITH AND AMERICA'S PRINCIPLES....................................24

APPENDIX III: CREATED EQUAL OR IDENTITY POLITICS?.....................29

APPENDIX IV: TEACHING AMERICANS ABOUT THEIR COUNTRY....34

I. INTRODUCTION

In the course of human events there have always been those who deny or reject human freedom, but Americans will never falter in defending the fundamental truths of human liberty proclaimed on July 4, 1776. We will—*we must*—always hold these truths.

The declared purpose of the President's Advisory 1776 Commission is to "enable a rising generation to understand the history and principles of the founding of the United States in 1776 and to strive to form a more perfect Union." This requires a restoration of American education, which can only be grounded on a history of those principles that is "accurate, honest, unifying, inspiring, and ennobling." And a rediscovery of our shared identity rooted in our founding principles is the path to a renewed American unity and a confident American future.

The Commission's first responsibility is to produce a report summarizing the principles of the American founding and how those principles have shaped our country. That can only be done by truthfully recounting the aspirations and actions of the men and women who sought to build America as a shining "city on a hill"—an exemplary nation, one that protects the safety and promotes the happiness of its people, as an example to be admired and emulated by nations of the world that wish to steer their government toward greater liberty and justice. The record of our founders' striving and the nation they built is our shared inheritance and remains a beacon, as Abraham Lincoln said, "not for one people or one time, but for all people for all time."

Today, however, Americans are deeply divided about the meaning of their country, its history, and how it should be governed. This division is severe enough to call to mind the disagreements between the colonists and King George, and those between the Confederate and Union forces in the Civil War. They amount to a dispute over not only the history of our country but also its present purpose and future direction.

The facts of our founding are not partisan. They are a matter of history. Controversies about the meaning of the founding can begin to be resolved by looking at the facts of our nation's founding. Properly understood, these facts address the concerns and aspirations of Americans of all social classes, income levels, races and religions, regions and walks of life. As well, these facts provide necessary—and wise—cautions against unrealistic hopes and checks against pressing partisan claims or utopian agendas too hard or too far.

Washington Crossing the Delaware
Emanuel Leutze

The principles of the American founding can be learned by studying the abundant documents contained in the record. Read fully and carefully, they show how the American people have ever pursued freedom and justice, which are the political conditions for living well. To learn this history is to become a better person, a better citizen, and a better partner in the American experiment of self-government.

Comprising actions by imperfect human beings, the American story has its share of missteps, errors, contradictions, and wrongs. These wrongs have always met resistance from the clear principles of the nation, and therefore our history is far more one of self-sacrifice, courage, and nobility. America's principles are named at the outset to be both universal—applying to everyone—and eternal: existing for all time. The remarkable American story unfolds under and because of these great principles.

Of course, neither America nor any other nation has perfectly lived up to the universal truths of equality, liberty, justice, and government by consent. But no

nation before America ever dared state those truths as the formal basis for its politics, and none has strived harder, or done more, to achieve them.

Lincoln aptly described the American government's fundamental principles as "a standard maxim for free society," which should be "familiar to all, and revered by all; constantly looked to, constantly labored for, and even though never perfectly attained, constantly approximated." But the very attempt to attain them—*every* attempt to attain them—would, Lincoln continued, constantly spread and deepen the influence of these

Martin Luther King Jr.

principles and augment "the happiness and value of life to all people of all colors everywhere." The story of America is the story of this ennobling struggle.

The President's Advisory 1776 Commission presents this first report with the intention of cultivating a better education among Americans in the principles and history of our nation and in the hope that a rediscovery of those principles and the forms of constitutional government will lead to a more perfect Union.

II. THE MEANING OF THE DECLARATION

The United States of America is in most respects a nation like any other. It embraces a people, who inhabit a territory, governed by laws administered by human beings. Like other countries, our country has borders, resources, industries, cities and towns, farms and factories, homes, schools, and houses of worship. And, although a relatively young country, its people have shared a history of common struggle and achievement, from carving communities out of a vast, untamed wilderness, to winning independence and forming a new government, through wars, industrialization,

waves of immigration, technological progress, and political change.

In other respects, however, the United States is unusual. It is a republic; that is to say, its government was designed to be directed by the will of the people rather than the wishes of a single individual or a narrow class of elites. Republicanism is an ancient form of government but one uncommon throughout history, in part because of its fragility, which has tended to make republics short-lived. Contemporary Americans tend to forget how historically rare republicanism has been, in part because of the success of republicanism in our time, which is derived in no small part from the very example and success of America.

In two decisive respects, the United States of America is unique. First, it has a definite birthday: July 4th, 1776. Second, it declares from the moment of its founding not merely the principles on which its new government will be based; it asserts those principles to be true and universal: "applicable to all men and all times," as Lincoln said.

Other nations may have birthdays. For instance, what would eventually evolve into the French Republic was born in 1789 when Parisians stormed a hated prison and launched the downfall of the French monarchy and its aristocratic regime. The Peoples Republic of China was born in 1949 when Mao Tse Tung's Chinese Communist Party defeated the Nationalists in the Chinese Civil War. But France and China as nations—as peoples and cultures inhabiting specific territories—stretch back centuries and even millennia, over the course of many governments.

There was no United States of America before July 4th, 1776. There was not yet, formally speaking, an American people. There were, instead, living in the thirteen British colonies in North America some two-and-a-half million *subjects* of a distant king. Those subjects became a people by declaring themselves such and then by winning the independence they had asserted as their right.

They made that assertion on the basis of principle, not blood or kinship or what we today might call "ethnicity." Yet this fact must be properly understood. As John Jay explained in *Federalist 2*,

Providence has been pleased to give this one connected country to one united people—a people descended from the same ancestors, speaking the same language, professing the same religion, attached to the same principles of government, very similar in their manners and customs, and who, by their joint counsels, arms, and efforts, fighting side by side throughout a long and bloody war, have nobly established general liberty and independence.

Yet, as Jay (and all the founders) well knew, the newly-formed American people were not *quite* as homogenous—in ancestry, language, or religion—as this statement would seem to assert. They were neither wholly English nor wholly Protestant nor wholly Christian. Some other basis would have to be found and asserted to bind the new people together and to which they would remain attached if they were to remain a people. That basis was the assertion of universal and eternal principles of justice and political legitimacy.

Declaration of Independence
John Trumbull

All honor to Jefferson-to the man who, in the concrete pressure of a struggle for national independence by a single people, had the coolness, forecast, and capacity to introduce into a merely revolutionary document, an abstract truth, applicable to all men and all times, and so to embalm it there, that to-day, and in all coming days, it shall be a rebuke and a stumbling-block to the very harbingers of re-appearing tyranny and oppression.

Abraham Lincoln

But this too must be qualified. Note that Jay lists six factors binding the American people together, of which principle is only one—the most important or decisive one, but still only one, and insufficient by itself. The American founders understood that, for republicanism to function and endure, a republican people must share a large measure of commonality in manners, customs, language, and dedication to the common good.

All states, all governments, make some claim to legitimacy—that is, an argument for why their existence and specific form are justified. Some dismiss all such claims to legitimacy as false, advanced to fool the ruled into believing that their rulers' actions are justified when in fact those actions only serve the private interests of a few.

But no actual government understands itself this way, much less makes such a cynical claim in public. All actual governments, rather, understand themselves as just and assert a public claim as to why. At the time of the American founding, the most widespread claim was a form of the divine right of kings, that is to say, the assertion that God appoints some men, or some families, to rule and consigns the rest to be ruled.

The American founders rejected that claim. As the eighteen charges leveled against King George in the Declaration of Independence make clear, our founders considered the British government of the time to be oppressive and unjust. They had no wish to replace the arbitrary government of one tyrant with that of another.

More fundamentally, having cast off their political connection to England, our founders needed to state a new principle of political legitimacy for their new government. As the Declaration of Independence puts

it, a "decent respect to the opinions of mankind" required them to explain themselves and justify their actions.

They did not merely wish to assert that they disliked British rule and so were replacing it with something they liked better. They wished to state a justification for their actions, and for the government to which it would give birth, that is both *true* and *moral:* moral because it is faithful to the truth about things.

Such a justification could only be found in the precepts of nature—specifically human nature—accessible to the human mind but not subject to the human will. Those precepts—whether understood as created by God or simply as eternal—are a given that man did not bring into being and cannot change. Hence the Declaration speaks of both "the Laws of Nature and of Nature's God"—it appeals to both reason and revelation—as the foundation of the underlying truth of the document's claims, and for the legitimacy of this new nation.

The core assertion of the Declaration, and the basis of the founders' political thought, is that "all men are created equal." From the principle of equality, the requirement for consent naturally follows: if all men are equal, then none may by right rule another without his consent.

The assertion that "all men are created equal" must also be properly understood. It does not mean that all human beings are equal in wisdom, courage, or any of the other virtues and talents that God and nature distribute unevenly among the human race. It means rather that human beings are equal in the sense that they are not by nature divided into castes, with natural rulers and ruled.

Thomas Jefferson liked to paraphrase the republican political thinker Algernon Sidney: "the mass of mankind has not been born with saddles on their backs, nor a favored few booted and spurred, ready to ride them legitimately, by the grace of God." Superiority of talent—even a superior ability to rule—is not a divine or natural title or warrant to rule. George Washington, surely one of the ablest statesmen who ever lived, never made such an outlandish claim and, indeed, vehemently rejected such assertions made by others about him.

As Abraham Lincoln would later explain, there was no urgent need for the founders to insert into a "merely revolutionary document" this "abstract truth, applicable to all men and all times." They could simply have told the British king they were separating and left it at that. But they enlarged the scope of their Declaration so that its principles would serve as "a rebuke and a stumbling-block to the very harbingers of re-appearing tyranny and oppression." The finality of the truth that "all men are created equal" was intended to make impossible any return to formal or legal inequality, whether to older forms such as absolute monarchy and hereditary aristocracy, or to as-yet-unimagined forms we have seen in more recent times.

which exist independently of government, whether government recognizes them or not. A bad government may deny or ignore natural rights and even prevent their exercise in the real world. But it can never negate or eliminate them.

The principles of the Declaration are universal and eternal. Yet they were asserted by a specific people, for a specific purpose, in a specific circumstance. The general principles stated in the document explain and justify the founders' particular actions in breaking off from Great Britain, and also explain the principles upon which they would build their new government. These principles apply to all men, but the founders acted to secure only Americans' rights, not those of all mankind. The world is still—and will always be—divided into nations, not all of which respect the rights of their people, though they should.

We confront, finally, the difficulty that the eternal principles elucidated in the Declaration were stated, and became the basis for an actual government, only a relatively short time ago. Yet if these principles are both eternal *and* accessible to the human mind, why were they not discovered and acted upon long before 1776?

> *When the architects of our republic wrote the magnificent words of the Constitution and the Declaration of Independence, they were signing a promissory note to which every American was to fall heir. This note was a promise that all men, yes, black men as well as white men, would be guaranteed the unalienable rights to life, liberty, and the pursuit of happiness.*
>
> Martin Luther King, Jr.

Natural equality requires not only the consent of the governed but also the recognition of fundamental human rights—including but not limited to life, liberty, and the pursuit of happiness—as well as the fundamental duty or obligation of all to respect the rights of others. These rights are found in nature and are not created by man or government; rather, men create governments to secure natural rights. Indeed, the very *purpose* of government is to secure these rights,

In a sense, the precepts of the American founders *were* known to prior thinkers, but those thinkers stated them in entirely different terms to fit the different political and intellectual circumstances of their times. For instance, ancient philosophers appear to teach that wisdom is a genuine title to rule and that in a decisive respect all men are *not* created equal. Yet they also teach that it is all but impossible for any actual, living man to attain genuine wisdom. Even if wisdom is a

legitimate title to rule, if perfect wisdom is unattainable by any living man, then no man is by right the ruler of any other except by their consent.

More fundamentally, by the time of the American founding, political life in the West had undergone two momentous changes. The first was the sundering of civil from religious law with the advent and widespread adoption of Christianity. The second momentous change was the emergence of multiple denominations within Christianity that undid Christian unity and in turn greatly undermined political unity. Religious differences became sources of political conflict and war. As discussed further in Appendix II, it was in response to these fundamentally new circumstances that the American founders developed the principle of religious liberty.

While the founders' principles are both true and eternal, they cannot be understood without also understanding that they were formulated by practical men to solve real-world problems. For the founders' solution to these problems we must turn to the Constitution.

III. A CONSTITUTION OF PRINCIPLES

It is one thing to discern and assert the true principles of political legitimacy and justice. It is quite another to establish those principles among an actual people, in an actual government, here on earth. As Winston Churchill put it in a not dissimilar context, even the best of men struggling in the most just of causes cannot guarantee victory; they can only deserve it.

The founders of the United States, perhaps miraculously, achieved what they set out to achieve. They defeated the world's strongest military and financial power and won their independence. They then faced the task of forming a country that would honor and implement the principles upon which they had declared their independence.

The bedrock upon which the American political system is built is the rule of law. The vast difference between tyranny and the rule of law is a central theme of political thinkers back to classical antiquity. The idea that the law is superior to rulers is the cornerstone of English constitutional thought as it developed over the centuries. The concept was transferred to the American colonies, and can be seen expressed throughout colonial pamphlets and political writings. As Thomas Paine reflected in *Common Sense*:

The safety of a republic depends essentially on the energy of a common national sentiment; on a uniformity of principles and habits; on the exemption of the citizens from foreign bias, and prejudice; and on that love of country which will almost invariably be found to be closely connected with birth, education and family.

Alexander Hamilton

For as in absolute governments the King is law, so in free countries the law ought to be king; and there ought to be no other. But lest any ill use should afterwards arise, let the crown at the conclusion of the ceremony be demolished, and scattered among the people whose right it is.

To assure such a government, Americans demanded a written legal document that would create both a structure and a process for securing their rights and liberties and spell out the divisions and limits of the powers of government. That legal document must be above ordinary legislation and day-to-day politics. That is what the founders meant by "constitution," and why our Constitution is "the supreme Law of the Land."

Their first attempt at a form of government, the Articles of Confederation and Perpetual Union, was adopted in the midst of the Revolutionary War and not ratified until 1781. During that time, American statesmen and citizens alike concluded that the Articles were too weak to fulfill a government's core functions. This consensus produced the Constitutional Convention of 1787, which met in Philadelphia that summer to write the document which we have today. It is a testament to those framers' wisdom and skill that the Constitution they produced remains the longest continually-operating written constitution in all of human history.

The meaning and purpose of the Constitution of 1787, however, cannot be understood without recourse to the principles of the Declaration of Independence—human equality, the requirement for government by consent, and the securing of natural rights—which the Constitution is intended to embody, protect, and nurture. Lincoln famously described the principles of the Declaration (borrowing from Proverbs 25:11) as an "apple of gold" and the Constitution as a "frame of silver" meant to "adorn and preserve" the apple. The latter was made for the former, not the reverse.

The form of the new government that the Constitution delineates is informed in part by the charges the Declaration levels at the British crown. For instance, the colonists charge the British king with failing to provide, or even interfering with, representative government; hence the Constitution provides for a representative legislature. It also charges the king with

concentrating executive, legislative, and judicial power into the same hands, which James Madison pronounced "the very definition of tyranny." Instead, the founders organized their new government into three coequal branches, checking and balancing the power of each against the others to reduce the risk of abuse of power.

Frederick Douglass

The intent of the framers of the Constitution was to construct a government that would be sufficiently strong to perform those essential tasks that only a government can perform (such as establishing justice, ensuring domestic tranquility, providing for the common defense, and promoting the general welfare—the main tasks named in the document's preamble), but not so strong as to jeopardize the people's liberties. In other words, the new government needed to be strong enough to have the power to *secure* rights without having so much power as to enable or encourage it to *infringe* rights.

More specifically, the framers intended the new Constitution to keep the thirteen states *united*—to prevent the breakup of the Union into two or more

smaller countries—while maintaining sufficient latitude and liberty for the individual states.

The advantages of union are detailed in the first fourteen papers of *The Federalist* (a series of essays written to urge the Constitution's adoption), and boil down to preventing and deterring foreign adventurism in North America, avoiding conflicts between threats, achieving economies of scale, and best utilizing the diverse resources of the continent.

While the Constitution is fundamentally a compact among the American people (its first seven words are "We the People of the United States"), it was ratified by special conventions in the states. The peoples of the states admired and cherished their state governments, all of which had adopted republican constitutions before a federal constitution was completed. Hence the framers of the new national government had to respect

For the founders, the principle that just government requires the consent of the governed in turn requires republicanism, because the chief way that consent is granted to a government on an ongoing basis is through the people's participation in the political process. This is the reason the Constitution "guarantee[s] to every State in this Union a Republican Form of Government."

Under the United States Constitution, the people are sovereign. But the people do not directly exercise their sovereignty, for instance, by voting directly in popular assemblies. Rather, they do so indirectly, through representative institutions. This is, on the most basic level, a practical requirement in a republic with a large population and extent of territory. But it is also intended to be a remedy to the defects common to all republics up to that time.

The framers of the Constitution faced a twofold

To throw obstacles in the way of a complete education is like putting out the eyes; to deny the rights of property is like cutting off the hands. To refuse political equality is to rob the ostracized of all self-respect, of credit in the market place, of recompense in the world of work, of a voice in choosing those who make and administer the law, a choice in the jury before whom they are tried, and in the judge who decides their punishment.

Elizabeth Cady Stanton

the states' prior existence and jealous guarding of their own prerogatives.

They also believed that the role of the federal government should be limited to performing those tasks that only a national government can do, such as providing for the nation's security or regulating commerce between the states, and that most tasks were properly the responsibility of the states. And they believed that strong states, as competing power centers, would act as counterweights against a potentially overweening central government, in the same way that the separation of powers checks and balances the branches of the federal government.

challenge. They had to assure those alarmed by the historical record that the new government was not *too republican* in simply copying the old, failed forms, while also reassuring those concerned about overweening centralized power that the government of the new Constitution was *republican enough* to secure equal natural rights and prevent the reemergence of tyranny.

The main causes of prior republican failure were class conflict and tyranny of the majority. In the simplest terms, the largest single faction in any republic would tend to band together and unwisely wield their numerical strength against unpopular minorities, leading to conflict and eventual collapse. The founders' primary remedy was union itself. Against the old idea

that republics had to be small, the founders countered that the very smallness of prior republics all but guaranteed their failure. In small republics, the majority can more easily organize itself into a dominant faction; in large republics, interests become too numerous for any single faction to dominate.

The inherent or potential partisan unwisdom of a dominant faction also would be tempered by representative government. Rather than the people acting as a body, the people would instead select officeholders to represent them. This would

refine and enlarge the public views, by passing them through the medium of a chosen body of citizens, whose wisdom may best discern the true interest of their country, and whose patriotism and love of justice will be least likely to sacrifice it to temporary or partial considerations. [Federalist 10]

And the separation of powers would work in concert with the principle of representation by incentivizing individual officeholders to identify their personal interests with the powers and prerogatives of their offices, and thus keep them alert to the danger of encroachments from other branches and offices.

The founders asserted that these innovations, and others, combined to create a republicanism that was at once old as well as new: true to the eternal principles and timeless ends of good government, but awake to and corrective of the deficiencies in prior examples of popular rule.

One important feature of our written constitution is the careful way that it *limits* the powers of each branch of government— that is, states what those branches may do, and by implication what they may *not* do. This is the real meaning of "limited government": not that the government's size or funding levels remain small, but that government's powers and activities must remain limited to certain carefully defined areas and responsibilities as guarded by bicameralism, federalism, and the separation of powers.

The Constitution was intended to endure. But because the founders well knew that no

document written by human beings could ever be perfect or anticipate every future contingency, they provided for a process to amend the document—but only by popular decision-making and not by ordinary legislation or judicial decree.

The first ten amendments, which would come to be known as the Bill of Rights, were included at the demand of those especially concerned about vesting the federal government with too much power and who wanted an enumeration of specific rights that the new government lawfully could not transgress. But all agreed that substantive rights are not granted by government; any just government exists only to secure these rights. And they specifically noted in the Ninth Amendment that the Bill of Rights was a selective and not an exclusive list; that is, the mere fact that a right is not mentioned in the Bill of Rights is neither proof nor evidence that it does not exist.

It is important to note the founders' understanding of three of these rights that are decisive for republican government and the success of the founders' project.

Our first freedom, religious liberty, is foremost a moral requirement of the natural freedom of the human mind. As discussed in Appendix II, it is also the indispensable solution to the political-religious problem that emerged in the modern world. Faith is both a matter of private conscience and public import, which is why the founders encouraged religious free exercise but barred the government from establishing any one national

Freedom is never more than one generation away from extinction. We didn't pass it to our children in the bloodstream. It must be fought for, protected, and handed on for them to do the same, or one day we will spend our sunset years telling our children and our children's children what it was once like in the United States where men were free.

Ronald Reagan

religion. The point is not merely to protect the state from religion but also to protect religion from the state so that religious institutions would flourish and pursue their divine mission among men.

Like religious liberty, freedom of speech and of the press is required by the freedom of the human mind. More plainly, it is a requirement for any government in which the people choose the direction of government policy. To choose requires public deliberation and debate. A people that cannot publicly express its opinions, exchange ideas, or openly argue about the course of its government is not free.

Finally, the right to keep and bear arms is required by the fundamental natural right to life: no man may justly be denied the means of his own defense. The political significance of this right is hardly less important. An armed people is a people capable of defending their liberty no less than their lives and is the last, desperate check against the worst tyranny.

IV. CHALLENGES TO AMERICA'S PRINCIPLES

Challenges to constitutional government are frequent and to be expected in a popular government based on consent. In his Farewell Address, George Washington advised his countrymen that when it came to the preservation of the Constitution they should "resist with care the spirit of innovation upon its principles however specious the pretexts." The Constitution has proven sturdy against narrow interest groups that seek to change elements of the Constitution merely to get their way.

At the same time, it is important to note that by design there is room in the Constitution for significant change and reform. Indeed, great reforms—like abolition, women's suffrage, anti-Communism, the Civil Rights Movement, and the Pro-Life Movement—have often come forward that improve our dedication to the principles of the Declaration of Independence under the Constitution.

More problematic have been movements that reject the fundamental truths of the Declaration of Independence and seek to destroy our constitutional order. The arguments, tactics, and names of these movements have changed, and the magnitude of the challenge has varied, yet they are all united by adherence to the same falsehood—that people do not have equal worth and equal rights.

At the infancy of our Republic, the threat was a despotic king who violated the people's rights and overthrew the colonists' longstanding tradition of self-government. After decades of struggle, the colonists succeeded in establishing a more perfect Union founded not upon the capricious whims of a tyrant, but republican laws and institutions founded upon self-evident and eternal truths.

It is the sacred duty of every generation of American patriots to defend this priceless inheritance.

SLAVERY

The most common charge levelled against the founders, and hence against our country itself, is that they were hypocrites who didn't believe in their stated principles, and therefore the country they built rests on a lie. This charge is untrue, and has done enormous damage, especially in recent years, with a devastating effect on our civic unity and social fabric.

Many Americans labor under the illusion that slavery was somehow a uniquely American evil. It is essential to insist at the outset that the institution be seen in a much broader perspective. It is very hard for people brought up in the comforts of modern America, in a time in which the idea that all human beings have inviolable rights and inherent dignity is almost taken for granted, to imagine the cruelties and enormities that were endemic in earlier times. But the unfortunate fact is that the institution of slavery has been more the rule than the exception throughout human history.

It was the Western world's repudiation of slavery, only just beginning to build at the time of the American Revolution, which marked a dramatic sea change in moral sensibilities. The American founders were living on the cusp of this change, in a manner that straddled two worlds. George Washington owned slaves, but came to detest the practice, and wished for "a plan adopted for the abolition of it." By the end of his life, he freed all the slaves in his family estate.

Thomas Jefferson also held slaves, and yet included in his original draft of the Declaration a strong condemnation of slavery, which was removed at the insistence of certain slaveholding delegates. Inscribed in marble at his memorial in Washington, D.C. is Jefferson's foreboding reference to the injustice of slavery: "I tremble for my country when I reflect that God is just; that His justice cannot sleep forever."

James Madison saw to it at the Constitutional Convention that, even when the Constitution compromised with slavery, it never used the word "slave" to do so. No mere semantics, he insisted that it was "wrong to admit in the Constitution the idea that there could be property in men."

Indeed, the compromises at the Constitutional Convention were just that: compromises. The three-fifths compromise was proposed by an antislavery delegate to prevent the South from counting their slaves as whole persons for purposes of increasing their congressional representation. The so-called fugitive slave clause, perhaps the most hated protection of all,

Abraham Lincoln

accommodated pro-slavery delegates but was written so that the Constitution did not sanction slavery in the states where it existed. There is also the provision in the Constitution that forbade any restriction of the slave trade for twenty years after ratification—at which time Congress immediately outlawed the slave trade.

The First Continental Congress agreed to discontinue the slave trade and boycott other nations that engaged in it, and the Second Continental Congress reaffirmed this policy. The Northwest Ordinance, a pre-Constitution law passed to govern the western territories (and passed again by the First Congress and signed into law by President Washington) explicitly bans slavery from those territories and from any states that might be organized there.

Above all, there is the clear language of the Declaration itself: "We hold these truths to be self-evident, that all men are created equal." The founders knew slavery was incompatible with *that* truth.

It is important to remember that, as a question of practical politics, no durable union could have been formed without a compromise among the states on the issue of slavery. Is it reasonable to believe that slavery could have been abolished sooner had the slave states not been in a union with the free? Perhaps. But what is momentous is that a people that included slaveholders founded their nation on the proposition that "all men are created equal."

So why did they say that without immediately abolishing slavery? To establish the principle of consent as the ground of all political legitimacy and to check against any possible future drift toward or return to despotism, for sure. But also, in Lincoln's words, "to declare the right, so that the enforcement of it might follow as fast as circumstances should permit."

The foundation of our Republic planted the seeds of the death of slavery in America. The Declaration's unqualified proclamation of human equality flatly contradicted the existence of human bondage and, along with the Constitution's compromises understood in light of that proposition, set the stage for abolition. Indeed, the movement to abolish slavery *that first began in the United States* led the way in bringing about the end of legal slavery.

Benjamin Franklin was president of the Pennsylvania Society for Promoting the Abolition of Slavery, and John Jay (the first Chief Justice of the Supreme Court) was the president of a similar society in New York. John Adams opposed slavery his entire life as a "foul contagion in the human character" and "an evil of colossal magnitude."

Frederick Douglass had been born a slave, but escaped and eventually became a prominent spokesman for the abolitionist movement. He initially condemned the Constitution, but after studying its history came to insist that it was a "glorious liberty document" and that the Declaration of Independence was "the ring-bolt to the chain of your nation's destiny."

And yet over the course of the first half of the 19th century, a growing number of Americans increasingly denied the truth at the heart of the founding. Senator John C. Calhoun of South Carolina famously rejected the Declaration's principle of equality as "the most dangerous of all political error" and a "self-evident lie." He never doubted that the founders meant what they said.

To this rejection, Calhoun added a new theory in which rights inhere not in every individual by "the Laws of Nature and of Nature's God" but in groups or races according to historical evolution. This new theory was developed to protect slavery—Calhoun claimed it was a

it was in the course of ultimate extinction," Abraham Lincoln observed in 1858. "All I have asked or desired anywhere, is that it should be placed back again upon the basis that the Fathers of our government originally placed it upon."

This conflict was resolved, but at a cost of more than 600,000 lives. Constitutional amendments were passed to abolish slavery, grant equal protection under the law, and guarantee the right to vote regardless of race. Yet the damage done by the denial of core American principles and by the attempted substitution of a theory of group rights in their place proved widespread and long-lasting. These, indeed, are the direct ancestors of some of the destructive theories that today divide our people and tear at the fabric of our country.

PROGRESSIVISM

In the decades that followed the Civil War, in response to the industrial revolution and the expansion of urban society, many American elites adopted a series of ideas to address these changes called Progressivism. Although not all of one piece, and not without its practical merits, the political thought of Progressivism held that the times had moved far beyond the founding era, and that contemporary society was too complex any longer to be governed by principles formulated in the 18th century. To use a contemporary analogy,

We live in an age of science and of abounding accumulation of material things. These did not create our Declaration. Our Declaration created them. The things of the spirit come first. Unless we cling to that, all our material prosperity, overwhelming though it may appear, will turn to a barren scepter in our grasp.

Calvin Coolidge

"positive good"—and specifically to prevent lawful majorities from stopping the spread of slavery into federal territories where it did not yet exist.

"In the way our Fathers originally left the slavery question, the institution was in the course of ultimate extinction, and the public mind rested in the belief that

Progressives believed that America's original "software"—the founding documents—were no longer capable of operating America's vastly more complex "hardware": the advanced industrial society that had emerged since the founding.

More significantly, the Progressives held that truths were not permanent but only relative to their time. They rejected the self-evident truth of the Declaration that all men are created equal and are endowed equally, either by nature or by God, with unchanging rights. As one prominent Progressive historian wrote in 1922, "To ask whether the natural rights philosophy of the Declaration of Independence is true or false, is essentially a meaningless question." Instead, Progressives believed there were only group rights that are constantly redefined and change with the times. Indeed, society has the power and obligation not only to define and grant new rights, but also to take old rights away as the country develops.

Based on this false understanding of rights, the Progressives designed a new system of government. Instead of securing fundamental rights grounded in nature, government—operating under a new theory of the "living" Constitution—should constantly evolve to secure evolving rights.

branch of government called at times the bureaucracy or the administrative state. This shadow government never faces elections and today operates largely without checks and balances. The founders always opposed government unaccountable to the people and without constitutional restraint, yet it continues to grow around us.

FASCISM

The principles of the Declaration have been threatened not only at home. In the 20th Century, two global movements threatened to destroy freedom and subject mankind to a new slavery. Though ideological cousins, the forces of Fascism and Communism were bitter enemies in their wars to achieve world domination. What united both totalitarian movements was their utter disdain for natural rights and free peoples.

> *Hold on, my friends, to the Constitution and to the Republic for which it stands. Miracles do not cluster, and what has happened once in 6,000 years, may not happen again. Hold on to the Constitution, because if the American Constitution should fail, there will be anarchy throughout the world.*
>
> Daniel Webster

In order to keep up with these changes, government would be run more and more by credentialed managers, who would direct society through rules and regulations that mold to the currents of the time. Before he became President of the United States, Woodrow Wilson laid out this new system whereby "the functions of government are in a very real sense independent of legislation, and even constitutions," meaning that this new view of government would operate independent of the people.

Far from creating an omniscient body of civil servants led only by "pragmatism" or "science," though, progressives instead created what amounts to a fourth

Fascism first arose in Italy under the dictatorship of Benito Mussolini, largely in response to the rise of Bolshevism in Russia. Like the Progressives, Mussolini sought to centralize power under the management of so-called experts. All power—corporate and political—would be exercised by the state and directed toward the same goal. Individual rights and freedoms hold no purchase under Fascism. Its principle is instead, in Mussolini's words, "everything in the State, nothing outside the State, nothing against the State." Eventually, Adolf Hitler in Germany wed this militant and dehumanizing political movement to his pseudo-scientific theory of Aryan racial supremacy, and Nazism was born.

The Nazi juggernaut quickly conquered much of Europe. The rule of the Axis Powers "is not a government based upon the consent of the governed," said President Franklin Delano Roosevelt. "It is not a union of ordinary, self-respecting men and women to protect themselves and their freedom and their dignity from oppression. It is an unholy alliance of power and pelf to dominate and enslave the human race."

Ronald Reagan speaking at the Brandenburg Gate

Before the Nazis could threaten America in our own hemisphere, the United States built an arsenal of democracy, creating more ships, planes, tanks, and munitions than any other power on earth. Eventually, America rose up, sending millions of troops across the oceans to preserve freedom.

Everywhere American troops went, they embodied in their own ranks and brought with them the principles of the Declaration, liberating peoples and restoring freedom. Yet, while Fascism died in 1945 with the collapse of the Axis powers, it was quickly replaced by a new threat, and the rest of the 20th century was defined by the United States' mortal and moral battle against the forces of Communism.

COMMUNISM

Communism seems to preach a radical or extreme form of human equality. But at its core, wrote Karl Marx, is "the idea of the class struggle as the immediate driving force of history, and particularly the class struggle between the bourgeois and the proletariat." In the communist mind, people are not born equal and free, they are defined entirely by their class.

Under Communism, the purpose of government is not to secure rights at all. Instead, the goal is for a "class struggle [that] necessarily leads to the dictatorship of the proletariat." By its very nature, this class struggle would be violent. "The Communists disdain to conceal their views and aims," Marx wrote. "They openly declare that their ends can be attained only by the forcible overthrow of all existing social conditions. Let the ruling classes tremble at a communist revolution."

This radical rejection of human dignity spread throughout much of the world. In Russia, the bloody Bolshevik Revolution during World War I established the communist Soviet Union. Communism understands itself as a universalist movement of global conquest, and communist dictatorships eventually seized power through much of Europe and Asia, and in significant parts of Africa and South America.

Led by the Soviet Union, Communism even threatened, or aspired to threaten, our liberties here at home. What it could not achieve through force of arms, it attempted through subversion. Communism did not succeed in fomenting revolution in America. But Communism's relentless anti-American, anti-Western, and atheistic propaganda did inspire thousands, and perhaps millions, to reject and despise the principles of our founding and our government. While America and its allies eventually won the Cold War, this legacy of anti-Americanism is by no means entirely a memory but still pervades much of academia and the intellectual and cultural spheres. The increasingly accepted economic theory of Socialism, while less violent than Communism, is inspired by the same flawed philosophy and leads down the same dangerous path of allowing the state to seize private property and redistribute wealth as the governing elite see fit.

For generations, America stood as a bulwark against global Communism. Our Cold War victory was owing not only to our superior technology, economy, and military. In the end, America won because the Soviet Union was built upon a lie. As President Ronald Reagan said, "I have seen the rise of Fascism and Communism.... But both theories fail. Both deny those God-given liberties that are the inalienable right of each person on this planet; indeed they deny the existence of God."

RACISM AND IDENTITY POLITICS

The Thirteenth Amendment to the Constitution, passed after the Civil War, brought an end to legal slavery. Blacks enjoyed a new equality and freedom, voting for and holding elective office in states across the Union. But it did not bring an end to racism, or to the unequal treatment of blacks everywhere.

Despite the determined efforts of the postwar Reconstruction Congress to establish civil equality for freed slaves, the postbellum South ended up devolving into a system that was hardly better than slavery. The system enmeshed freedmen in relationships of extreme dependency, and used poll taxes, literacy tests, and the violence of vigilante groups like the Ku Klux Klan to prevent them from exercising their civil rights, particularly the right to vote. Jim Crow laws enforced the strict segregation of the races, and gave legal standing in some states to a pervasive subordination of blacks.

It would take a national movement composed of people from different races, ethnicities, nationalities, and religions to bring about an America fully committed to ending legal discrimination.

The Civil Rights Movement culminated in the 1960s with the passage of three major legislative reforms affecting segregation, voting, and housing rights. It presented itself, and was understood by the American people, as consistent with the principles of the founding. "When the architects of our republic wrote the magnificent words of the Constitution and the Declaration of Independence, they were signing a promissory note to which every American was to fall

heir," Martin Luther King, Jr. said in his "I Have a Dream" speech. "This note was a promise that all men, yes, black men as well as white men, would be guaranteed the unalienable rights to life, liberty, and the pursuit of happiness."

It seemed, finally, that America's nearly two-century effort to realize fully the principles of the Declaration had reached a culmination. But the heady spirit of the original Civil Rights Movement, whose leaders forcefully quoted the Declaration of Independence, the Constitution, and the rhetoric of the founders and of Lincoln, proved to be short-lived.

The Civil Rights Movement was almost immediately turned to programs that ran counter to the lofty ideals of the founders. The ideas that drove this change had been growing in America for decades, and they distorted many areas of policy in the half century that followed. Among the distortions was the abandonment of nondiscrimination and equal opportunity in favor of "group rights" not unlike those advanced by Calhoun and his followers. The justification for reversing the promise of color-blind civil rights was that past discrimination requires present effort, or affirmative action in the form of preferential treatment, to overcome long-accrued inequalities. Those forms of preferential treatment built up in our system over time, first in administrative rulings, then executive orders, later in congressionally passed law, and finally were sanctified by the Supreme Court.

Civil Rights March on Washington, D.C.

Today, far from a regime of equal natural rights for equal citizens, enforced by the equal application of law, we have moved toward a system of explicit group privilege that, in the name of "social justice," demands equal results and explicitly sorts citizens into "protected classes" based on race and other demographic categories.

Eventually this regime of formal inequality would come to be known as "identity politics." The stepchild of earlier rejections of the founding, identity politics

today our country is in danger of throwing this inheritance away.

The choice before us now is clear. Will we choose the truths of the Declaration? Or will we fall prey to the false theories that have led too many nations to tyranny? It is our mission—all of us—to restore our national unity by rekindling a brave and honest love for our country and by raising new generations of citizens who not only know the self-evident truths of our founding, but act worthy of them.

Promote, then, as an object of primary importance, institutions for the general diffusion of knowledge. In proportion as the structure of a government gives force to public opinion, it is essential that public opinion should be enlightened.

George Washington

(discussed in Appendix III) values people by characteristics like race, sex, and sexual orientation and holds that new times demand new rights to replace the old. This is the opposite of King's hope that his children would "live in a nation where they will not be judged by the color of their skin but by the content of their character," and denies that all are endowed with the unalienable rights to life, liberty, and the pursuit of happiness.

Identity politics makes it less likely that racial reconciliation and healing can be attained by pursuing Martin Luther King, Jr.'s dream for America and upholding the highest ideals of our Constitution and our Declaration of Independence.

V.   THE TASK OF NATIONAL RENEWAL

All the good things we see around us—from the physical infrastructure, to our high standards of living, to our exceptional freedoms—are direct results of America's unity, stability, and justice, all of which in turn rest on the bedrock of our founding principles. Yet

This great project of national renewal depends upon true education—not merely training in particular skills, but the formation of citizens. To remain a free people, we must have the knowledge, strength, and virtue of a free people. From families and schools to popular culture and public policy, we must teach our founding principles and the character necessary to live out those principles.

This includes restoring patriotic education that teaches the truth about America. That doesn't mean ignoring the faults in our past, but rather viewing our history clearly and wholly, with reverence and love. We must also prioritize personal responsibility and fulfilling the duties we have toward one another as citizens. Above all, we must stand up to the petty tyrants in every sphere who demand that we speak only of America's sins while denying her greatness. At home, in school, at the workplace, and in the world, it is the people—and only the people—who have the power to stand up for America and defend our way of life.

THE ROLE OF THE FAMILY

By their very nature, families are the first educators, teaching children how to treat others with respect, make wise decisions, exercise patience, think for themselves, and steadfastly guard their God-given liberties. It is good mothers and fathers, above all others, who form good people and good citizens.

This is why America's founding fathers often echoed the great Roman statesman Cicero in referring to the family as the "seminary of the republic." They understood that the habits and morals shaped in the home determine the character of our communities and the ultimate fate of our country.

When children see their mother and father hard at work, they learn the dignity of labor and the reward of self-discipline. When adults speak out against dangerous doctrines that threaten our freedoms and values, children learn the time-tested concept of free expression and the courageous spirit of American independence. When parents serve a neighbor in need, they model charity and prove that every human being has inherent worth. And when families pray together, they acknowledge together the providence of the Almighty God who gave them their sacred liberty.

For the American republic to endure, families must remain strong and reclaim their duty to raise up morally responsible citizens who love America and embrace the gifts and responsibilities of freedom and self-government.

TEACHING AMERICA

The primary duty of schools is to teach students the basic skills needed to function in society, such as reading, writing, and mathematics. As discussed in Appendix IV, our founders also recognized a second and essential task: educators must convey a sense of enlightened patriotism that equips each generation with a knowledge of America's founding principles, a deep reverence for their liberties, and a profound love of their country.

Make no mistake: The love we are talking about is something different from romantic or familial love, something that cannot be imposed by teachers or schools or government edicts, least of all in a free country. Like any love worthy of the name, it must be embraced freely and be strong and unsentimental enough to coexist with the elements of disappointment, criticism, dissent, opposition, and even shame that come with moral maturity and open eyes. But it is love all the same, and without the deep foundation it supplies, our republic will perish.

State and local governments—not the federal government—are responsible for adopting curricula that teach children the principles that unite, inspire, and ennoble all Americans. This includes lessons on the Revolutionary War, the Declaration of Independence, and the Constitutional Convention. Educators should teach an accurate history of how the permanent principles of America's founding have been challenged and preserved since 1776. By studying America's true heritage, students learn to embrace and preserve the triumphs of their forefathers while identifying and avoiding their mistakes.

States and school districts should reject any curriculum that promotes one-sided partisan opinions, activist propaganda, or factional ideologies that demean America's heritage, dishonor our heroes, or deny our principles. Any time teachers or administrators promote political agendas in the classroom, they abuse their platform and dishonor every family who trusts them with their children's education and moral development.

"Law and liberty cannot rationally become the object of our love," wrote founding father James Wilson, "unless they first become the objects of our knowledge." Students who are taught to understand America's exceptional principles and America's powerful history grow into strong citizens who respect the rule of law and protect the country they know and love.

A SCHOLARSHIP OF FREEDOM

Universities in the United States are often today hotbeds of anti-Americanism, libel, and censorship that combine to generate in students and in the broader culture at the very least disdain and at worst outright hatred for this country.

The founders insisted that universities should be at the core of preserving American republicanism by instructing students and future leaders of its true basis and instilling in them not just an understanding but a reverence for its principles and core documents. Today, our higher education system does almost the precise opposite. Colleges peddle resentment and contempt for American principles and history alike, in the process

and historical truth, shames Americans by highlighting only the sins of their ancestors, and teaches claims of systemic racism that can only be eliminated by more discrimination, is an ideology intended to manipulate opinions more than educate minds.

Deliberately destructive scholarship shatters the civic bonds that unite all Americans. It silences the discourse essential to a free society by breeding division, distrust, and hatred among citizens. And it is the intellectual force behind so much of the violence in our cities, suppression of free speech in our universities, and defamation of our treasured national statues and symbols.

To restore our society, academics must return to their vocation of relentlessly pursuing the truth and engaging in honest scholarship that seeks to understand the world and America's place in it.

THE AMERICAN MIND

Americans yearn for timeless stories and noble heroes that inspire them to be good, brave, diligent, daring, generous, honest, and compassionate.

> *To place before mankind the common sense of the subject, in terms so plain and firm as to command their assent, and to justify ourselves in the independent stand we are compelled to take. . . . it was intended to be an expression of the American mind, and to give to that expression the proper tone and spirit called for by the occasion.*
>
> Thomas Jefferson

weakening attachment to our shared heritage.

In order to build up a healthy, united citizenry, scholars, students, and all Americans must reject false and fashionable ideologies that obscure facts, ignore historical context, and tell America's story solely as one of oppression and victimhood rather than one of imperfection but also unprecedented achievement toward freedom, happiness, and fairness for all. Historical revisionism that tramples honest scholarship

Millions of Americans devour histories of the American Revolution and the Civil War and thrill to the tales of Washington, Jefferson, Hamilton, and Franklin, Lincoln and Grant, Sojourner Truth and Frederick Douglass. We still read the tales of Hawthorne and Melville, Twain and Poe, and the poems of Whitman and Dickinson. On Independence Day, we hum John Philip Sousa's "Stars and Stripes Forever" and sing along to Woody Guthrie's "This Land is Your Land." Americans applaud the loyalty, love, and kindness

shared by the March sisters in *Little Women*, revere the rugged liberty of the cowboys in old westerns, and cheer the adventurous spirit of young Tom Sawyer. These great works have withstood the test of time because they speak to eternal truths and embody the American spirit.

It is up to America's artists, authors, filmmakers, musicians, social media influencers, and other culture leaders to carry on this tradition by once again giving shape and voice to America's self-understanding—to be what Jefferson called "an expression of the American mind."

To them falls the creative task of writing stories, songs, and scripts that help to restore every American's conviction to embrace the good, lead virtuous lives, and act with an attitude of hope toward a better and bolder future for themselves, their families, and the entire nation.

REVERENCE FOR THE LAWS

The principles of equality and consent mean that all are equal before the law. No one is above the law, and no one is privileged to ignore the law, just as no one is outside the law in terms of its protection.

In his Lyceum Address, a young Abraham Lincoln warned of two results of a growing disregard for the rule of law. The first is mob rule: "whenever the vicious portion of [our] population shall be permitted to gather in bands of hundreds and thousands, and burn churches, ravage and rob provision stores, throw printing-presses into rivers, shoot editors, and hang and burn obnoxious persons at pleasure and with impunity, depend upon it, this government cannot last."

But Lincoln also warned of those of great ambition who thirst for distinction and, although "he would as willingly, perhaps more so, acquire it by doing good as harm, yet, that opportunity being past, and nothing left to be done in the way of building up, he would set boldly to the task of pulling down."

Whether of the Left or of the Right, both mob rule and tyrannical rule violate the rule of law because both are rule by the base passions rather than the better angels of

our nature. Both equally threaten our constitutional order.

When crimes go unpunished or when good men do nothing, the lawless in spirit will become lawless in practice, leading to violence and demagoguery.

Patriotic education must have at its center a respect for the rule of law, including the Declaration and the Constitution, so that we have what John Adams called "a government of laws, and not of men."

In the end, Lincoln's solution must be ours:

Let every American, every lover of liberty, every well-wisher to his posterity, swear by the blood of the Revolution, never to violate in the least particular, the laws of the country; and never to tolerate their violation by others. As the patriots of seventy-six did to the support of the Declaration of Independence, so to the support of the Constitution and Laws, let every American pledge his life, his property, and his sacred honor;-let every man remember that to violate the law, is to trample on the blood of his father, and to tear the character of his own, and his children's liberty. Let reverence for the laws, be breathed by every American mother, to the lisping babe, that prattles on her lap-let it be taught in schools, in seminaries, and in colleges; let it be written in Primers, spelling books, and in Almanacs;-let it be preached from the pulpit, proclaimed in legislative halls, and enforced in courts of justice.

VI. CONCLUSION

On the 150th Anniversary of the signing of the Declaration of Independence, President Calvin Coolidge raised the immortal banner in his time. "It is often asserted," he said, "that the world has made a great deal of progress since 1776 ... and that we may therefore very well discard their conclusions for something more modern. But that reasoning cannot be applied to this great charter. If all men are created equal, that is final. If they are endowed with inalienable rights, that is final. If governments derive their just powers from the consent of the governed, that is final. No advance, no progress can be made beyond these propositions."

America's founding principles are true not because any generation—including our own—has lived them perfectly, but because they are based upon the eternal truths of the human condition. They are rooted in our capacity for evil and power for good, our longing for truth and striving for justice, our need for order and our love of freedom. Above all else, these principles recognize the worth, equality, potential, dignity, and glory of each and every man, woman, and child created in the image of God.

Throughout our history, our heroes—men and women, young and old, black and white, of many faiths and from all parts of the world—have changed America for the better not by abandoning these truths, but by appealing to them. Upon these universal ideals, they built a great nation, unified a strong people, and formed a beautiful way of life worth defending.

To be an American means something noble and good. It means treasuring freedom and embracing the vitality of self-government. We are shaped by the beauty, bounty, and wildness of our continent. We are united by the glory of our history. And we are distinguished by the American virtues of openness, honesty, optimism, determination, generosity, confidence, kindness, hard work, courage, and hope. Our principles did not create these virtues, but they laid the groundwork for them to grow and spread and forge America into the most just and glorious country in all of human history.

As we approach the 250th anniversary of our independence, we must resolve to teach future generations of Americans an accurate history of our country so that we all learn and cherish our founding principles once again. We must renew the pride and gratitude we have for this incredible nation that we are blessed to call home.

When we appreciate America for what she truly is, we know that our Declaration is worth preserving, our Constitution worth defending, our fellow citizens worth loving, and our country worth fighting for.

It is our task now to renew this commitment. So we proclaim, in the words our forefathers used two and a half centuries ago, "for the support of this Declaration, with a firm reliance on the protection of divine Providence, we mutually pledge to each other our Lives, our Fortunes, and our sacred Honor."

The Declaration of Independence is the ring-bolt to the chain of your nation's destiny; so, indeed, I regard it. The principles contained in that instrument are saving principles. Stand by those principles, be true to them on all occasions, in all places, against all foes, and at whatever cost.

Frederick Douglass

APPENDIX I

THE DECLARATION OF INDEPENDENCE

IN CONGRESS, JULY 4, 1776

The unanimous Declaration of the thirteen united States of America,

When in the Course of human events, it becomes necessary for one people to dissolve the political bands which have connected them with another, and to assume among the powers of the earth, the separate and equal station to which the Laws of Nature and of Nature's God entitle them, a decent respect to the opinions of mankind requires that they should declare the causes which impel them to the separation.

We hold these truths to be self-evident, that all men are created equal, that they are endowed by their Creator with certain unalienable Rights, that among these are Life, Liberty and the pursuit of Happiness.-That to secure these rights, Governments are instituted among Men, deriving their just powers from the consent of the governed, -That whenever any Form of Government becomes destructive of these ends, it is the Right of the People to alter or to abolish it, and to institute new Government, laying its foundation on such principles and organizing its powers in such form, as to them shall seem most likely to effect their Safety and Happiness. Prudence, indeed, will dictate that Governments long established should not be changed for light and transient causes; and accordingly all experience hath shewn, that mankind are more disposed to suffer, while evils are sufferable, than to right themselves by abolishing the forms to which they are accustomed. But when a long train of abuses and usurpations, pursuing invariably the same Object evinces a design to reduce them under absolute Despotism, it is their right, it is their duty, to throw off such Government, and to provide new Guards for their future security.-Such has been the patient sufferance of these Colonies; and such is now the necessity which constrains them to alter their former Systems of Government. The history of the present King of Great Britain is a history of repeated injuries and usurpations, all having in direct object the establishment of an absolute Tyranny over these States. To prove this, let Facts be submitted to a candid world.

He has refused his Assent to Laws, the most wholesome and necessary for the public good.

He has forbidden his Governors to pass Laws of immediate and pressing importance, unless suspended in their operation till his Assent should be obtained; and when so suspended, he has utterly neglected to attend to them.

He has refused to pass other Laws for the accommodation of large districts of people, unless those people would relinquish the right of Representation in the Legislature, a right inestimable to them and formidable to tyrants only.

He has called together legislative bodies at places unusual, uncomfortable, and distant from the depository of their public Records, for the sole purpose of fatiguing them into compliance with his measures.

He has dissolved Representative Houses repeatedly, for opposing with manly firmness his invasions on the rights of the people.

He has refused for a long time, after such dissolutions, to cause others to be elected; whereby the Legislative powers, incapable of Annihilation, have returned to the People at large for their exercise; the State remaining in the meantime exposed to all the dangers of invasion from without, and convulsions within.

He has endeavored to prevent the population of these States; for that purpose obstructing the Laws for Naturalization of Foreigners; refusing to pass others to encourage their migrations hither, and raising the conditions of new Appropriations of Lands.

He has obstructed the Administration of Justice, by refusing his Assent to Laws for establishing Judiciary powers.

He has made Judges dependent on his Will alone, for the tenure of their offices, and the amount and payment of their salaries.

He has erected a multitude of New Offices, and sent hither swarms of Officers to harass our people, and eat out their substance.

He has kept among us, in times of peace, Standing Armies without the Consent of our legislatures.

He has affected to render the Military independent of and superior to the Civil power.

He has combined with others to subject us to a jurisdiction foreign to our constitution, and unacknowledged by our laws; giving his Assent to their Acts of pretended Legislation:

For Quartering large bodies of armed troops among us:

For protecting them, by a mock Trial, from punishment for any Murders which they should commit on the Inhabitants of these States:

For cutting off our Trade with all parts of the world:

For imposing Taxes on us without our Consent:

For depriving us in many cases, of the benefits of Trial by Jury:

For transporting us beyond Seas to be tried for pretended offences

For abolishing the free System of English Laws in a neighboring Province, establishing therein an Arbitrary government, and enlarging its Boundaries so as to render it at once an example and fit instrument for introducing the same absolute rule into these Colonies:

For taking away our Charters, abolishing our most valuable Laws, and altering fundamentally the Forms of our Governments:

For suspending our own Legislatures, and declaring themselves invested with power to legislate for us in all cases whatsoever.

He has abdicated Government here, by declaring us out of his Protection and waging War against us.

He has plundered our seas, ravaged our Coasts, burnt our towns, and destroyed the lives of our people.

He is at this time transporting large Armies of foreign Mercenaries to complete the works of death, desolation and tyranny, already begun with circumstances of Cruelty & perfidy scarcely paralleled in the most barbarous ages, and totally unworthy the Head of a civilized nation.

He has constrained our fellow Citizens taken Captive on the high Seas to bear Arms against their Country, to become the executioners of their friends and Brethren, or to fall themselves by their Hands.

He has excited domestic insurrections amongst us, and has endeavored to bring on the inhabitants of our frontiers, the merciless Indian Savages, whose known rule of warfare, is an undistinguished destruction of all ages, sexes and conditions.

In every stage of these Oppressions We have Petitioned for Redress in the most humble terms: Our repeated Petitions have been answered only by repeated injury. A Prince whose character is thus marked by every act which may define a Tyrant, is unfit to be the ruler of a free people.

Nor have We been wanting in attentions to our British brethren. We have warned them from time to time of attempts by their legislature to extend an unwarrantable jurisdiction over us. We have reminded them of the circumstances of our emigration and settlement here. We have appealed to their native justice and magnanimity, and we have conjured them by the ties of our common kindred to disavow these usurpations, which, would inevitably interrupt our connections and correspondence. They too have been deaf to the voice of justice and of consanguinity. We must, therefore, acquiesce in the necessity, which denounces our Separation, and hold them, as we hold the rest of mankind, Enemies in War, in Peace Friends.

We, therefore, the Representatives of the united States of America, in General Congress, Assembled, appealing to the Supreme Judge of the world for the rectitude of our intentions, do, in the Name, and by Authority of the good People of these Colonies, solemnly publish and declare, That these United Colonies are, and of Right ought to be Free and Independent States; that they are Absolved from all Allegiance to the British Crown, and that all political connection between them and the State of Great Britain, is and ought to be totally dissolved; and that as Free and Independent States, they have full Power to levy War, conclude Peace, contract Alliances, establish Commerce, and to do all other Acts and Things which Independent States may of right do. And for the support of this Declaration, with a firm reliance on the protection of divine Providence, we mutually pledge to each other our Lives, our Fortunes and our sacred Honor.

APPENDIX II
FAITH AND AMERICA'S PRINCIPLES

History underscores the overwhelming importance of religious faith in American life, but some today see religious practice and political liberty to be in conflict and hold that religion is divisive and should be kept out of the public square. The founders of America held a very different view. They not only believed that all people have a right to religious liberty but also that religious faith is indispensable to the success of republican government. "The God who gave us life, gave us liberty at the same time," Thomas Jefferson once wrote. "The hand of force may destroy, but cannot disjoin them."

The idea that faith sustains the principles of equality and natural rights is deeply rooted in American society and proven through human experience. The social, political, and personal value of religious faith within America's public space has been recognized and honored from the start. "Of all the dispositions and habits which lead to political prosperity, Religion and morality are indispensable supports," George Washington observed in his Farewell Address. "In vain would that man claim the tribute of Patriotism, who should labor to subvert these great Pillars of human happiness, these firmest props of the duties of Men and citizens." He went on to warn:

> *Let us with caution indulge the supposition, that morality can be maintained without religion. Whatever may be conceded to the influence of refined education on minds of peculiar structure, reason and experience both forbid us to expect that National morality can prevail in exclusion of religious principle.*

CIVIL AND RELIGIOUS LIBERTY

By the time of the American founding, political life in the West had undergone two momentous changes. The first was the sundering of civil from religious law. Prior to the widespread adoption of Christianity, Western societies made no distinction between civil and religious law, between the demands of the state and the demands of the gods. Laws against murder and theft, for instance, had the same status as laws compelling religious observance, and all laws were enforced by the same political institutions. Pagan societies recognized no "private sphere" of conscience into which the state may not justly intrude.

Christianity overturned this unity by separating political from religious obligation and making the latter primarily a matter of faith, superintended by a church whose authority was extrinsic to civil law. Thus began a millennium of tension and conflict between secular and ecclesiastical authorities.

The second momentous change was the emergence of multiple sects within Christianity. In the pre-Christian world, all subjects or citizens of any given political community were expected to believe in and worship the same God or gods by the same rites and ceremonies. This basic unity held through the first several centuries of Christianity. But the Great Schism and, more significantly, the Reformation, undid Christian unity, which in turn greatly undermined political unity. Religious differences became sources of political conflict and war. The nations of Europe fell into internal sectarian divisions and external religious-political wars.

British monarchs not only disputed one another's claims to the throne but imposed their preferred religious doctrines on the whole nation. Gruesome tortures and political imprisonments were common. The Puritans proclaimed a "commonwealth" which executed the Anglican king. The executed king's son proceeded to supplant the "commonwealth," but because his brother was suspected of being Catholic, Protestants expelled him in the so-called

"Glorious Revolution" of 1688 that installed the Protestant monarch of the Netherlands and his wife as England's king and queen.

In the 17th century, religious believers of many stripes came to North America as refugees from Europe's religious persecutions. Ironically, the most famous attempt to form a separate religious community—the Pilgrims' relocation to Massachusetts—eventually led to the core American principle of religious liberty.

THE FOUNDERS' SOLUTION

The founders were ever mindful of the religious oppression and persecution that had existed throughout history. They knew that religious zeal often leads to the assumption that specific beliefs should be "established" by governments, meaning certain religious doctrines should be enforced by law as the official religion of the state. Individuals who are not members of that religious body and do not accept its teachings often did not enjoy the same rights as a result. Discriminations against nonbelievers ranged from mild to the most awful, but the "establishment" of one religious body by government always divided the population into privileged and non-privileged classes, resulting in endless bitter struggles for religious dominance.

At the same time, the founders recognized man's natural yearning to pursue the truth about God and freely practice the teachings inspired by those religious beliefs. They knew that religious beliefs, good for the ultimate happiness of the individual, were also good for politics because they encouraged the virtues (such as justice, self-restraint, courage, and truthfulness) necessary for self-government. To violate the consciences of citizens by using force to change their religious beliefs was a gross injustice. Violations of conscience by government would not strengthen the attachment of citizens to their government but would only foster hypocrisy, hatred, and rebellion.

The American founders did not claim to settle the ultimate questions of reason and revelation. But for the first time in history, the founders believed they saw a *practicable* and just alternative to religious persecution and conflict. Unlike previous forms of government, the Constitution they framed did not include the power to "establish" a national religion, and it specifically denied that anyone could be prevented from holding office by a "religious test." They underlined this by *expressly* forbidding the federal government in the First Amendment from "establishing" any religion and, to make it even clearer, guaranteeing the free exercise of religion.

Together, these provisions give religious liberty primacy among the natural rights secured by our Constitution. This follows from the principles of the Declaration, as the foremost way individuals fulfill their well-being—in exercising their natural right to "the pursuit of happiness"—is through the religious teachings and institutions they believe and hope will lead to their salvation.

We often use the phrase "the separation of church and state" to refer to the founders' practical settlement of these questions, but this phrase is usually misunderstood to mean a complete separation of religion and politics, which is a very different idea. When the founders denied government the power to establish a religion, they did not intend to expunge religion from political life but to make room for the religious beliefs and free expression of all citizens.

THE COMMON GROUND OF REASON AND REVELATION

The founders emphasized where the moral teachings of religious faith and the ground of political liberty were in agreement. Just as they were confident that government has no theological expertise to decide the path to

salvation, they were equally confident that a well-designed republican constitution is sanctioned by human nature and open to moral reasoning shared among human beings.

General moral precepts can be understood by human reason, and faith echoes these precepts. In other words, when the Declaration of Independence opens by appealing to "the Laws of Nature and of Nature's God," it means that there is a human morality accessible to both reason and revelation. This is the common moral ground of the American founding, where reason and revelation work together for civil and religious liberty. Consider this from the Reverend Samuel Cooper in 1780:

> We want not, indeed, a special revelation from heaven to teach us that men are born equal and free; that no man has a natural claim of dominion over his neighbors. . . . These are the plain dictates of that reason and common sense with which the common parent of men has informed the human bosom. It is, however, a satisfaction to observe such everlasting maxims of equity confirmed, and impressed upon the consciences of men, by the instructions, precepts, and examples given us in the sacred oracles; one internal mark of their divine original, and that they come from him "who hath made of one blood all nations to dwell upon the face of the earth." [Acts 17:26]

In proclaiming the self-evident truths of the Declaration, the founders interwove reason and revelation into America's creed. One such truth is that there are fixed laws higher than those enacted by governments. Reason and faith secure limits on the reach of man-made laws, thereby opening up the space for civil and religious liberty. Another is that, in the act of creation, however conceived, all came into existence as equals: the Creator gives no person or group a higher right to rule others without their agreement. Yet another is that all are gifted through their human nature with intrinsic rights which they cannot sign away, above all the great rights of "Life, Liberty, and the Pursuit of Happiness." In all of these things, *the founders limited the ends of government in order to open up the higher ends of man.*

The purpose of the founders' ingenious division of church and state was neither to weaken the importance of faith nor to set up a secular state, but to open up the public space of society to a common American morality. Religious institutions, which were influential before the American Revolution, became powerful witnesses for the advancement of equality, freedom, opportunity, and human dignity.

- The American Revolution might not have taken place or succeeded without the moral ideas spread through the pulpits, sermons, and publications of Christian instructors. On the nation's 150th Independence Day celebration, President Calvin Coolidge said that the principles of the Declaration of Independence were

  > found in the text, the sermons and the writings of the early colonial clergy who were earnestly undertaking to instruct their congregations in the great mystery of how to live. They preached equality because they believed in the fatherhood of God and the brotherhood of man. They justified freedom by the text that we are all created in the divine image, all partakers of the divine spirit.

- Even before the eighteenth century, Quakers and the faithful of other denominations, drawing on the Bible and on philosophy, began a crusade to abolish race-based slavery in the colonies. Anti-slavery literature was largely faith-based and spread through the free states via churches. One of the most famous anti-slavery writers in history, Harriet Beecher Stowe, was the devout daughter of a great American reformist clergyman and wife of a well-known theologian. Her worldwide best-seller, *Uncle Tom's Cabin*, fired the moral indignation of millions that helped lay the ground for abolition.

- America's greatest reform movements have been founded or promoted by religious leaders and laypersons reared in faithful home environments. Mother Elizabeth Ann Seton in the early nineteenth century set up orphanages and established free schools for poor girls. The tireless effort to end Jim Crow and extend civil and voting rights to African Americans and other minorities was driven by clergy and lay faithful of a multitude of denominations, including most prominently the Reverend Martin Luther King, Jr., who used nonviolent tactics to advocate for equal rights. The Pro-Life Movement today is led by clergy and the faithful of virtually every denomination.

- Local religious leaders have been a key buttress supporting our communities. Neighborhood and parish churches, temples, and mosques still are the strongest organized centers of help for the local poor, jobless, homeless, and families down on their luck. For generations, neighbors have assisted neighbors through church networks, helping the needy avoid the dehumanization of prolonged dependency on government welfare. Today, countless men and women actively feed and care for the poor, house and speak for immigrants and the disadvantaged, minister to jailed and released criminals, and advocate powerfully for a better society and a more peaceful world, supported by the charitable funding of Americans of all faiths.

- Clergy of various denominations have sacrificed career goals and risked their lives in order to minister to men and women serving in the armed forces. The brave soldiers who protect America against foreign dangers depend on the corps of military chaplains who help cultivate the warriors' courage, inner strength, and perseverance they need to succeed in their missions. Religious chaplains open every session of Congress, and clergy pray at presidential inaugurals, state funerals, and other official occasions.

CONCLUSION

The United States has journeyed far since its founding. While the founders certainly had disagreements about the nature of religion, they had little doubt that faith was essential to the new experiment in self-government and republican constitutionalism. They knew that citizens who practiced the faith under the protection of religious liberty would support the Constitution that embodies their rights.

The shared morality of faithful citizens would sustain a republican culture that would foster stable family relationships and encourage important virtues like fortitude to defend the nation in war, self-restraint over physical appetites or lust for wealth, compassion toward neighbors and strangers in need, self-disciplined labor, intellectual integrity, independence from long-term reliance on private or public benefits, justice in all relationships, prudence in judging the common good, courage to defend their rights and liberties, and finally, piety towards the Creator whose favor determines the well-being of society.

We have arrived at a point where the most influential part of our nation finds these old faith-based virtues dangerous, useless, or perhaps even laughable. At the same time, many Americans feel that we have veered off the path that has brought so many happiness and success, and fear a growing factionalism cannot be overcome merely by electing a different president or political party. How can America overcome this partisan divide?

The answer to this rising concern must begin by frankly and humbly admitting that the common ground of equal natural rights on which our common morality is based is no longer visible to many Americans. We must refocus on the proposition that united this nation from the beginning: the proposition of the Declaration of Independence that there are "self-evident truths" which unite all Americans under a common creed.

But it is almost impossible to hold to this creed—which describes what and who we *are*—without reference to the Creator as the ultimate source of human equality and natural rights. This is the deepest reason why the founders saw faith as the key to good character as well as good citizenship, and why we must remain "one Nation under God, indivisible, with liberty and justice for all."

The proposition of political equality is powerfully supported by biblical faith, which confirms that all human beings are equal in dignity and created in God's image. Every form of religious faith is entitled to religious liberty, so long as all comprehend and sincerely assent to the fundamental principle that under "the Laws of Nature and of Nature's God" all human beings are equally endowed with unalienable rights to life, liberty, and the pursuit of happiness. As the first American president wrote in 1790 to the Hebrew Congregation in Newport, Rhode Island:

> The Citizens of the United States of America have a right to applaud themselves for having given to mankind examples of an enlarged and liberal policy: a policy worthy of imitation. All possess alike liberty of conscience and immunities of citizenship. It is now no more that toleration is spoken of, as if it was by the indulgence of one class of people, that another enjoyed the exercise of their inherent natural rights. For happily the Government of the United States, which gives to bigotry no sanction, to persecution no assistance, requires only that they who live under its protection should demean themselves as good citizens, in giving it on all occasions their effectual support.

APPENDIX III
CREATED EQUAL OR IDENTITY POLITICS?

Americans are deeply committed to the principle of equality enshrined in the Declaration of Independence, that all are created equal and equally endowed with natural rights to life, liberty, and the pursuit of happiness. This creed, as Abraham Lincoln once noted, is "the electric cord" that "links the hearts of patriotic and liberty-loving" people everywhere, no matter their race or country of origin. The task of American civic education is to transmit this creed from one generation of Americans to the next.

In recent times, however, a new creed has arisen challenging the original one enshrined in the Declaration of Independence. This new creed, loosely defined as identity politics, has three key features. First, the creed of identity politics defines and divides Americans in terms of collective social identities. According to this new creed, our racial and sexual identities are more important than our common status as individuals equally endowed with fundamental rights.

Second, the creed of identity politics ranks these different racial and social groups in terms of privilege and power, with disproportionate moral worth allotted to each. It divides Americans into two groups: oppressors and victims. The more a group is considered oppressed, the more its members have a moral claim upon the rest of society. As for their supposed oppressors, they must atone and even be punished in perpetuity for their sins and those of their ancestors.

Third, the creed of identity politics teaches that America itself is to blame for oppression. America's "electric cord" is not the creed of liberty and equality that connects citizens today to each other and to every generation of Americans past, present, and future. Rather, America's "electric cord" is a heritage of oppression that the majority racial group inflicts upon minority groups, and identity politics is about assigning and absolving guilt for that oppression.

According to this new creed, Americans are not a people defined by their dedication to human equality, but a people defined by their perpetuation of racial and sexual oppression.

THE HISTORICAL PRECEDENT FOR IDENTITY POLITICS

Whereas the Declaration of Independence founded a nation grounded on human equality and equal rights, identity politics sees a nation defined by oppressive hierarchies. But this vision of America is actually not new. While identity politics may seem novel and ground-breaking, it resurrects prior attempts in American history to deny the meaning of equality enshrined in the Declaration. In portraying America as racist and white supremacist, identity politics advocates follow Lincoln's great rival Stephen A. Douglas, who wrongly claimed that American government "was made on the white basis" "by white men, for the benefit of white men." Indeed, there are uncanny similarities between 21st century activists of identity politics and 19th century apologists for slavery.

John C. Calhoun is perhaps the leading forerunner of identity politics. Rejecting America's common political identity that follows from the Declaration's principles, he argued that the American polity was not an actual

community at all but was reducible only to diverse majority and minority groups. Calhoun saw these groups as more or less permanent, slowly evolving products of their race and particular historical circumstances.

Like modern-day proponents of identity politics, Calhoun believed that achieving unity through rational deliberation and political compromise was impossible; majority groups would only use the political process to oppress minority groups. In Calhoun's America, respect for each group demanded that each hold a veto over the actions of the wider community. But Calhoun also argued that some groups must outrank others in the majoritarian decision-making process. In Calhoun's America, one minority group—Southern slaveholders—could veto any attempt by the majority group—Northern States—to restrict or abolish the enslavement of another group. In the context of American history, *the original form of identity politics was used to defend slavery.*

As American history teaches, dividing citizens into identity groups, especially on the basis of race, is a recipe for stoking enmity among all citizens. It took the torrent of blood spilled in the Civil War and decades of subsequent struggles to expunge Calhoun's idea of group hierarchies from American public life. Nevertheless, activists pushing identity politics want to resuscitate a modified version of his ideas, rejecting the Declaration's principle of equality and defining Americans once again in terms of group hierarchies. They aim to make this the defining creed of American public life, and they have been working for decades to bring it about.

INTELLECTUAL ORIGINS OF IDENTITY POLITICS

The modern revival of identity politics stems from mid-20th century European thinkers who sought the revolutionary overthrow of their political and social systems but were disillusioned by the working class's lack of interest in inciting revolution. This setback forced revolutionaries to reconsider their strategy.

One of the most prominent, the Italian Marxist Antonio Gramsci, argued that the focus should not be on economic revolution as much as taking control of the institutions that shape culture. In Gramsci's language, revolutionaries should focus on countering the "Hegemonic Narrative" of the established culture with a "Counter-Narrative," creating a counter-culture that subverts and seeks to destroy the established culture.

Gramsci was an important influence on the thinkers of the "Frankfurt School" in Germany, who developed a set of revolutionary ideas called Critical Theory. Herbert Marcuse, one member of the Frankfurt School who immigrated to the United States in the 1940s, became the intellectual godfather of American identity politics. With little hope that the white American worker could be coaxed to revolution, Marcuse focused not on instigating class conflict but on instigating cultural conflicts around racial identity. He saw revolutionary potential in "the substratum of the outcasts and outsiders, the exploited and persecuted of other races and other colors."

These ideas led to the development of Critical Race Theory, a variation of critical theory applied to the American context that stresses racial divisions and sees society in terms of minority racial groups oppressed by the white majority. Equally significant to its intellectual content is the role Critical Race Theory plays in promoting fundamental social transformation. Following Gramsci's strategy of taking control of the culture, Marcuse's followers use the approach of Critical Race Theory to impart an oppressor-victim narrative upon generations of Americans. This work of cultural revolution has been going on for decades, and its first political reverberations can be seen in 1960s America.

THE RADICALIZATION OF AMERICAN POLITICS IN THE 1960S

Prior to the 1960s, movements in American history that sought to end racial and sexual discrimination, such as abolition, women's suffrage, or the Civil Rights Movement, did so on the ground set by the Declaration of Independence.

In leading the Civil Rights Movement, Martin Luther King, Jr., was aware that other, more revolutionary groups wanted to fight in terms of group identities. In his "I Have a Dream" speech, King rejected hateful stereotyping based on a racialized group identity. The "marvelous new militancy which has engulfed the Negro community must not lead us to distrust all white people," he warned. King refused to define Americans in terms of permanent racialized identities and called on Americans "to lift our nation from the quicksands of racial injustice to the solid rock of brotherhood" and see ourselves as one nation united by a common political creed and commitment to Christian love.

"When the architects of our republic wrote the magnificent words of the Constitution and the Declaration of Independence, they were signing a promissory note to which every American was to fall heir," King wrote. "This note was a promise that all men, yes, black men as well as white men, would be guaranteed the unalienable rights to life, liberty, and the pursuit of happiness."

As the 1960s advanced, however, many rejected King's formulation of civil rights and reframed debates about equality in terms of racial and sexual identities. The Civil Rights Movement came to abandon the nondiscrimination and equal opportunity of colorblind civil rights in favor of "group rights" and preferential treatment. A radical women's liberation movement reimagined America as a patriarchal system, asserting that every woman is a victim of oppression by men. The Black Power and black nationalist movements reimagined America as a white supremacist regime. Meanwhile, other activists constructed artificial groupings to further divide Americans by race, creating new categories like "Asian American" and "Hispanic" to teach Americans to think of themselves in terms of group identities and to rouse various groups into politically cohesive bodies.

THE INCOMPATIBILITY OF IDENTITY POLITICS WITH AMERICAN PRINCIPLES

Identity politics divide Americans by placing them perpetually in conflict with each other. This extreme ideology assaults and undermines the American principle of equality in several key ways.

First, identity politics attacks American self-government. Through the separation of powers and the system of checks and balances, American constitutionalism prevents any one group from having complete control of the government. In order to form a majority, the various groups that comprise the nation must resolve their disagreements in light of shared principles and come to a deliberative consensus over how best to govern. In the American system, public policy is decided by prudential compromise among different interest groups for the sake of the common good.

Identity politics, on the other hand, sees politics as the realm of permanent conflict and struggle among racial, gender, and other groups, and no compromise between different groups is possible. Rational deliberation and compromise only preserve the oppressive status quo. Instead, identity politics relies on humiliation, intimidation, and

coercion. American self-government, where all citizens are equal before the law, is supplanted by a system where certain people use their group identity to get what they want.

Second, by dividing Americans into oppressed and oppressor groups, activists of identity politics propose to punish some citizens – many times for wrongs their ancestors allegedly committed – while rewarding others. Members of oppressed groups must ascend, and members of oppressor groups must descend. This new system denies that human beings are endowed with the same rights, and creates new hierarchies with destructive assumptions and practices.

On the one hand, members of oppressed groups are told to abandon their shared civic identity as Americans and think of themselves in terms of their sexual or racial status. The consequence is that they should no longer see themselves as agents responsible for their own actions but as victims controlled by impersonal forces. In a word, they must reject, not affirm, the Declaration's understanding of self-government according to the consent of the governed. If members of oppressed groups want to become free, they must rely upon a regime of rewards and privileges assigned according to group identity.

On the other hand, members of oppressor groups merit public humiliation at the hands of others. Diversity training programs, for example, force members of "oppressor" groups to confess before their co-workers how they contribute to racism. Educational programs based on identity politics often use a person's race to degrade or ostracize them.

These degradations of individuals on the basis of race expose the lie that identity politics promotes the equal protection of rights. Advocates of identity politics argue that all hate speech should be banned but then define hate speech as only applying to protected identity groups who are in turn free to say whatever they want about their purported oppressors. This leads to a "cancel culture" that punishes those who violate the terms of identity politics.

Third, identity politics denies the fundamental moral tenet of the Declaration, that human beings are equal by nature. This founding principle provides a permanent and immutable standard for remedying wrongs done to Americans on the basis of race, sex, or any group identity.

Repudiating this universal tenet, activists pushing identity politics rely instead on cultural and historical generalizations about which groups have stronger moral claims than others. They claim this approach offers a superior and more historically sensitive moral standard. But unlike the standard based on a common humanity—what Lincoln called "an abstract truth, applicable to all men and all times"—their historical standard is not permanent. Rather, it adjusts to meet the political fashions of a particular moment. By this standard, ethnicities that were once considered "oppressed" can in short order turn into "oppressors," and a standard that can turn a minority from victim to villain within the course of a few years is no standard at all.

Fourth, identity-politics activists often are radicals whose political program is fundamentally incompatible not only with the principles of the Declaration of Independence but also the rule of law embodied by the United States Constitution. Antagonism to the creed expressed in the Declaration seems not an option but a necessary part of their strategy. When activists are discussing seemingly innocuous campaigns to promote "diversity," they are often aiming for fundamental structural change.

CONCLUSION

Identity politics is fundamentally incompatible with the principle of equality enshrined in the Declaration of Independence.

Proponents of identity politics rearrange Americans by group identities, rank them by how much oppression they have experienced at the hands of the majority culture, and then sow division among them. While not as barbaric or dehumanizing, this new creed creates new hierarchies as unjust as the old hierarchies of the antebellum South, making a mockery of equality with an ever-changing scale of special privileges on the basis of racial and sexual identities. The very idea of equality under the law—of one nation sharing King's "solid rock of brotherhood"—is not possible and, according to this argument, probably not even desirable.

All Americans, and especially all educators, should understand identity politics for what it is: rejection of the principle of equality proclaimed in the Declaration of Independence. As a nation, we should oppose such efforts to divide us and reaffirm our common faith in the fundamental equal right of every individual to life, liberty, and the pursuit of happiness.

APPENDIX IV
TEACHING AMERICANS ABOUT THEIR COUNTRY

America's founders understood the importance of education to the long-term success or failure of the American experiment in self-government. Liberty and learning are intimately intertwined and rely on each other for protection and nurturing. As James Madison noted, "What spectacle can be more edifying or more seasonable, than that of Liberty and Learning, each leaning on the other for their mutual and surest support?"

Education in civics, history, and literature holds the central place in the well-being of both students and communities. For republican government, citizens with such an education are essential. The knowledge of human nature and unalienable rights—understanding what it means to be human—brings a deeper perspective to public affairs, for the simple reason that educated citizens will take encouragement or warning from our past in order to navigate the present.

A wholesome education also passes on the stories of great Americans from the past who have contributed their genius, sacrifices, and lives to build and preserve this nation. They strengthen the bond that a vast and diverse people can point to as that which makes us one community, fostered by civil political conversation and a shared and grateful memory.

The crucial contribution that a quality civics education makes to the well-being of America and its citizens is love for our country, properly understood. A healthy attachment to this country—true patriotism—is neither blind to its flaws nor fanatical in believing that America is the source of all good. Rather, the right sort of love of country holds it up to an objective standard of right and wrong, with the desire and intent that the country do what is right. Where the country has done what is good, citizens justly praise those who came before them. Where it has done wrong, they should criticize the country and work to make sure that we—the people who govern it—do what is right.

Rather than cast aside the serious study of America's founding principles or breed contempt for America's heritage, our educational system should aim to teach students about the true principles and history of their country— a history that is "accurate, honest, unifying, inspiring, and ennobling."

THE MISUSE OF HISTORY

To begin such an education, we must first avoid an all-too-common mistake. It is wrong to think of history by itself as the standard for judgment. The standard is set by unchanging principles that transcend history. Our founders called these "self-evident truths" and published these truths for all the world to see in the Declaration of Independence: there are "Laws of Nature and of Nature's God" that inform human interactions, all human beings are created equal, and all human beings have fundamental rights that are theirs as human beings, not the gift of government.

Consider the subject of slavery. At the time the Declaration was written, between fifteen and twenty percent of the American people were held as slaves. This brutal, humiliating fact so contradicted the principles of equality and liberty announced in 1776 that many people now make the mistake of denouncing equality and liberty. Yet as we condemn slavery now, we learn from the founders' public statements and private letters that they condemned it then. One great reason they published the Declaration's bold words was to show that slavery is a

wrong according to nature and according to God. With this Declaration, they started the new nation on a path that would lead to the end of slavery. As Abraham Lincoln explained, the founding generation was in no position to end this monstrous crime in one stroke, but they did mean "to declare the right, so that the enforcement of it might follow as fast as circumstances should permit."

The point is this: The key to freedom for all is discovered in the moral standard proclaimed in the Declaration. It would, the founders hoped, prove to be the key that would unlock the door to equality and liberty for all. *History* tells the story of how our country has succeeded—and at times failed—in living up to the standard of right and wrong. Our task as citizens in a national community is to live—and it is the task of teachers to teach—so as to keep our community in line with our *principles*.

The purpose of genuine, liberal education is to come to know what it means to be free. Education seeks knowledge of the nature of things, especially of human nature and of the universe as a whole. Man is that special part of the universe that seeks to know where we stand within it. We wonder about its origins. The human person is driven by a yearning for self-knowledge, seeking to understand the essential nature and purpose of his or her life and what it means to carry that life out in relationship with others.

The surest guides for this quest to understand freedom and human nature are the timeless works of philosophy, political thought, literature, history, oratory, and art that civilization has produced. Contrary to what is sometimes claimed, these works are not terribly difficult to identify: they are marked by their foundational and permanent character and their ability to transcend the time and landscape of their creation. No honest, intelligent surveyor of human civilization could deny the unique brilliance of Homer or Plato, Dante or Shakespeare, Washington or Lincoln, Melville or Hawthorne.

But far too little of this guidance is given in American classrooms today. In most K-12 social studies and civics classes, serious study of the principles of equality and liberty has vanished. The result has been a rising generation of young citizens who know little about the origins and stories of their country, and less about the true standards of equality and liberty. This trend is neither new nor unreported, but it is leaving a terrible and growing void as students suffer from both the ignorance of not realizing what they lack, and a certain arrogance that they have no need to find out.

THE DECLINE OF AMERICAN EDUCATION

This pronounced decline of American education began in the late nineteenth century when progressive reformers began discarding the traditional understanding of education. The old understanding involved conveying a body of transcendent knowledge and practical wisdom that had been passed down for generations and which aimed to develop the character and intellect of the student. The new education, by contrast, pursued contradictory goals that are at the same time mundane and unrealistically utopian.

In the view of these progressive educators, human nature is ever-changing, so the task of the new education was to remake people in order to improve the human condition. They sought to reshape students in the image they thought best, and education became an effort to engineer the way students think.

This new education deemed itself "pragmatic," subordinating America's students to the demands of the new industrial economy for skills-based, jobs-oriented training. Rather than examine the past for those unchanging truths and insights into our shared humanity, students today are taught to assume that the founders' views were narrow and deficient: *that's just how people used to think, but we know better now.*

Under this new approach, the only reason to study the works of Aristotle, Shakespeare, or America's founders is not to learn how to be virtuous, self-governing citizens, not to learn anything true, good, or beautiful, but to realize how such figures of yesteryear are unfit for the present day. Such a vision of education teaches that ideas evolve as human progress marches on, as supposedly old and worn ideas are cast aside on the so-called "wrong side of history."

This new education replaced humane and liberal education in many places, and alienated Americans from their own nature, their own identities, and their own place and time. It cuts students off from understanding that which came before them. Like square pegs and round holes, students are made to fit the latest expert theory about where history is headed next.

As the twentieth century continued, these progressive views reached their logical apex: there is no ultimate or objective truth, only various expressions of different cultures' beliefs. Wittingly or unwittingly, progressives concluded that truth is an ideological construct created by those with inordinate wealth and power to further their own particular agendas. In such a relativist environment, progressive education may as well impose its own ideological construct on the future. They did not call it indoctrination, but that is what it is.

Since the 1960s, an even more radicalized challenge has emerged. This newer challenge arrived under the feel-good names of "liberation" and "social justice." Instead of offering a comprehensive, unifying human story, these ideological approaches diminish our shared history and disunite the country by setting certain communities against others. History is no longer tragic but melodramatic, in which all that can be learned from studying the past is that groups victimize and oppress each other.

By turning to bitterness and judgment, distorted histories of those like Howard Zinn or the journalists behind the "1619 Project" have prevented their students from learning to think inductively with a rich repository of cultural, historical, and literary referents. Such works do not respect their students' independence as young thinkers trying to grapple with social complexity while forming their empirical judgments about it. They disdain today's students, just as they doubt the humanity, goodness, or benevolence in America's greatest historical figures. They see only weaknesses and failures, teaching students truth is an illusion, that hypocrisy is everywhere, and that power is all that matters.

A few reforms of note have been attempted to improve America's civic educational system, but they fail to address the key problems.

The first was embraced with good intentions. Common Core appeared to be a promising way for the federal government to supply a framework to improve the nation's schools. But the Constitution leaves education to the states and localities and denies the federal government any authority to impose what it wants to be taught in the nation's schools. To surmount this obstacle, the federal government used significant federal funding to entice states to adopt Common Core. Nevertheless, within a few years it became clear that students in states that "voluntarily" adopted Common Core suffered significantly lower academic performance and fewer marketable skills than comparable cohorts of students who had been educated outside the Common Core regime. This system of micromanaged "standards" proved to be a recipe for bureaucratic control and sterile conformity instead of a pathway towards better instruction. We learned from the failed Common Core experiment that one-size-fits-all national models are a blueprint for trivializing and mechanizing learning.

A more recently proposed remedy is called the "New Civics" (or "Action Civics"). The progressive approach to education rests on the faulty notion that knowledge concerning long-term human and social concerns is divided between "facts" (scientific data separated from judgments about right and wrong) and "values" (preferences about moral matters, such as justice, which are said to have no objective status). Most students, yearning to make the world better, find the study of "facts" boring and meaningless. The New Civics approach is to prioritize a values-oriented praxis over fact-based knowledge. As a result, New Civics uses direct community service and political action (such as protesting for gun control or lobbying for laws to address climate change) to teach students to bring change to the system itself. Under this guise, civics education becomes less about teaching civic knowledge and more about encouraging contemporary policy positions.

However well-intended, the New Civics only aggravates the already inherent problems of progressive education. Dispensing with ideas that transcend and inform history, students lack criteria for judging what a politically healthy nation looks like and they cannot defend what practical actions actually would improve the health of their community. A well-formulated education in political and moral principles is the necessary source of the knowledge citizens need to make wise judgments about voting, demonstrating, or any other civic activity. By neglecting true civic education, the New Civics movement only compounds the mistakes of today's conventional education in civics.

WHAT IS AUTHENTIC EDUCATION?

There are many aspects of formal education. The importance of professional education and technical training is not here in dispute. There is no question that one crucial purpose of education is to equip individuals with the knowledge and skills they need to provide for themselves and their families. More fundamental is the broader and deeper education called liberal education.

Education liberates human beings in the true sense—liberation from ignorance and confusion, from prejudice and delusion, and from untamed passions and fanciful hopes that degrade and destroy us as civilized persons. It helps us see the world clearly and honestly. In revealing human nature, it reveals what is right and good for human beings: authentic education is not "value-neutral" but includes moral education that explains the standards for right and wrong. It takes up the hard but essential task of character formation. Such an education can form free men and free women—self-reliant and responsible persons capable of governing themselves as individuals and taking part in self-government.

Such an education starts by teaching that all Americans are equal members of one national community. The unique character and talents of each person should be recognized and developed. The wide experiences and the varied backgrounds of our citizens should be respected and honored. But the truths that equality and liberty belong by nature to every human being without exception must be taught as the moral basis of civic friendship, economic opportunity, citizenship, and political freedom.

Such an education respects students' intelligence and thirst for the truth. It is unafraid both to focus on the contributions made by the exceptional few, or acknowledge those that are less powerful, less fortunate, weaker, or marginalized. With the principle of equality as a foundation, such an education can incorporate the study of injustice and of tragedy in human affairs—including the American story's uglier parts—and patiently addresses the ways injustices can be corrected.

Rather than learning to hate one's country or the world for its inevitable wrongs, the well-educated student learns to appreciate and cherish the oases of civilization: solid family structures and local communities; effective,

representative, and limited government; the rule of law and the security of civil rights and private property; a love of the natural world and the arts; good character and religious faith.

In the American context, an essential purpose of this honest approach is to encourage citizens to embrace and cultivate love of country. Thoughtful citizens embrace their national community not only because it is their own, but also because they see what it can be at its best. Just as students know their family members have good qualities and flaws, good education will reckon the depths and heights of our common history.

GENUINE CIVICS EDUCATION

Civics and government classes should rely almost exclusively on primary sources. Primary sources link students with the real events and persons they are studying. The writings, speeches, first-hand accounts, and documents of those who were acting out the drama of history open a genuine communication, mediated by the written word, between historical figures and students that can bring to life the past. Primary sources without selective editing also allow students to study principles and arguments unfiltered by present-day historians' biases and agendas.

It is important for students to learn the reasons America's founders gave for building our country as they did. Students should learn and contemplate what the founders' purposes, hopes, and greatest concerns truly were, and primary sources will help them begin these considerations. Students should not read the Declaration of Independence as archaeology but as the idea that animates our nation with claims that are true for all time. As Alexander Hamilton reminds us in one of those primary documents (his 1775 essay *Farmer Refuted*),

> The sacred rights of mankind are not to be rummaged for, among old parchments, or musty records. They are written, as with a sun beam, in the whole volume of human nature, by the hand of the divinity itself; and can never be erased or obscured by mortal power.

Civics and government classes ought to teach students about the philosophical principles and foundations of the American republic, including natural law, natural rights, human equality, liberty, and constitutional self-government. Students should learn the reasons why our constitutional order is structured as a representative democracy and why a constitutional republic includes such features as the separation of powers, checks and balances, and federalism. They should study the benefits and achievements of our constitutional order, the Civil War's challenge to that order, and the ways the Constitution has been changed—not only by amendment and not always for the better—over the course of time. Finally, these classes ought to culminate in the student's understanding and embracing the responsibilities of good citizenship.

A genuine civics education focuses on fundamental questions concerning the American experiment in self-government. The best way to proceed is for the teacher to assign core original documents to students to read as carefully and thoroughly as they are able and then initiate age-appropriate discussion to surface and consider the meaning of the document. Teachers will find that students of every age have a genuine interest in engaging in discussion (and disagreement) about what these documents say, because they soon realize these enduring words speak to their own lives and experiences.

Using the Declaration of Independence, the Constitution, and the *Federalist Papers*, the following are a few examples of prompts teachers can use to encourage civics discussion amongst students:

- What does human equality mean in the statement that "all men are created equal"? Equal in what respects? What view of human nature does this presuppose? Does the Declaration intend to include African Americans, as Abraham Lincoln, Frederick Douglass, and Martin Luther King, Jr., all insisted?

- What does the Declaration mean by asserting that all persons possess rights that are not "alienable"? Who or what, precisely, can alienate our rights? Are all rights deemed inalienable, or only some? And if the latter, why are they different?

- Why did the founding generation consider government's powers to be "just" only when government is instituted by the consent of the governed? Is justice for the founders based on nothing more than consent? What considerations might be more authoritative than consent?

- At the time the *Federalist Papers* were being written, the new Constitution did not include the Bill of Rights. What are the rights and protections enumerated in the Bill of Rights and how did they come to be amendments to the Constitution?

- Why did the founders opt for representative democracy over the "pure" version of democracy practiced in ancient Athens? How do the two kinds of democracy differ? What did the *Federalist* assert was the inadequacy of ancient democracy?

- How does the Constitution seek to reconcile democracy, which means rule by the majority, with the rights of minorities? Stated differently, how does the Constitution do justice both to the equality of all and to the liberty of each? What exactly is the difference between a democracy and republic?

- What economic conditions make American democracy possible? Could American democracy under the Constitution be reconciled with any and every economic system? Why does the Constitution protect property rights? Why do critics of American democracy such as Karl Marx believe that private property (protected by our Constitution) is the root of injustice? How would Madison and Hamilton have responded to Marx and his followers' criticisms?

- Students should read the best-known speeches and writings of progressive presidents Woodrow Wilson, Theodore Roosevelt, and Franklin Roosevelt on economic democracy. In what ways do they differ from the principles and structure of the Constitution? Would the Constitution need to be significantly amended to fit their proposals? Apart from amendments, in what other ways has progressivism changed our constitutional system?

- Implicit in these questions are other basic documents and major speeches that every American citizen should study. The questions concerning the meaning of human equality, inalienable rights, popular consent, and the right of revolution call for a fresh examination—in the light of the Declaration—of such key works as Frederick Douglass's speech on "The Meaning of the Fourth of July to the Negro" and Chief Justice Taney's infamous opinion for the Supreme Court majority in *Dred Scott v. Sandford* (holding that African-Americans "had no rights which the white man was bound to respect"). Douglass's and Lincoln's scathing criticisms of Taney's pro-slavery opinion should be taught with these as well.

- Students should read the 1848 Seneca Falls "Declaration of Sentiments and Resolutions" calling for women's suffrage, and Dr. Martin Luther King, Jr.'s "I Have a Dream" speech. Why did Elizabeth Cady Stanton look to the form and substance of the Declaration of Independence in crafting the Seneca Falls Declaration? What did King mean in asserting that the Declaration of Independence and the Constitution constituted a "promissory note to which every American was to fall heir"?

These questions cover just a sample of the issues that come to the fore as students read the primary documents of the founding and history of America. Other less fundamental but still important documents, speeches, and topics could be added. Recognizing that political activism has no place in formal education, mock civics and community service projects should be encouraged.

CONCLUSION

Among the virtues to be cultivated in the American republic, the founders knew that a free people must have a knowledge of the principles and practices of liberty, and an appreciation of their origins and challenges.

While this country has its imperfections, just like any other country, in the annals of history the United States has achieved the greatest degree of personal freedom, security, and prosperity for the greatest proportion of its own people and for others around the world. These results are the good fruit of the ideas the founding generation expressed as true for all people at all times and places.

An authentic civics education will help rebuild our common bonds, our mutual friendship, and our civic devotion. But we cannot *love* what we do not *know*.

This is why civics education, education relating to the citizen, must begin with knowledge, which is, as George Washington reminds us, "the surest basis of public happiness."

THE PRESIDENT'S ADVISORY 1776 COMMISSION

Larry P. Arnn, Chair
Carol Swain, Vice Chair
Matthew Spalding, Executive Director

Phil Bryant
Jerry Davis
Michael Farris
Gay Hart Gaines
John Gibbs
Mike Gonzalez
Victor Davis Hanson
Charles Kesler
Peter Kirsanow
Thomas Lindsay
Bob McEwen
Ned Ryun
Julie Strauss

Ex-officio Members
Michael Pompeo, Secretary of State
Christopher C. Miller, Acting Secretary of Defense
David L. Bernhardt, Secretary of the Interior
Ben Carson, Secretary of Housing and Urban Development
Mitchell M. Zais, Acting Secretary of Education
Brooke Rollins, Assistant to the President for Domestic Policy
Doug Hoelscher, Assistant to the President for Intergovernmental Affairs

The Commission is grateful to the following individuals who assisted with the preparation of the 1776 Report: William Bock, Alexandra Campana, Ariella Campana, Joshua Charles, Brian Morgenstern, Macy Mount, McKenzie Snow, and Alec Torres.

Adam Honeysett, *Designated Federal Officer.*

The 1776 *Report*

The President's Advisory 1776 Commission

CPSIA information can be obtained
at www.ICGtesting.com
Printed in the USA
BVHW020435160721
612047BV00001B/8

9 781952 615221